KV-639-031

I2133163

Bitter Vengeance

After Mark Kennick saw his entire family murdered by five killers hired by Seth Corby, he made a promise to his father that he would avenge their deaths. Even though he had never handled a gun in his life, Mark bought a couple of Colts and strapped them on.

Only a chance meeting with a stranger saved Mark's life when he was called out in the saloon. That stranger was Frank Calhoun, an outlaw with a price on his head and four bounty hunters on his trail. In a secret hide-out in the hills with Calhoun and his granddaughter, Stella, Mark learned how to handle his guns.

He vowed to practise day after day under Calhoun's critical eye, until he would be fast enough to exact his revenge on Corby and his gunhawks.

Bitter Vengeance

Max Chartair

A Black Horse Western

ROBERT HALE · LONDON

© John Glasby 2006
First published in Great Britain 2006

ISBN-10: 0-7090-8191-X
ISBN-13: 978-0-7090-8191-3

Robert Hale Limited
Clerkenwell House
Clerkenwell Green
London EC1R 0HT

The right of John Glasby to be identified as
author of this work has been asserted by him
in accordance with the Copyright, Designs and
Patents Act 1988

SANDWELL LIBRARY & INFORMATION SERVICE	
I2133163	
Bertrams	01.01.07
W	£11.25

Typeset by
Derek Doyle & Associates, Shaw Heath
Printed and bound in Great Britain by
Antony Rowe Limited, Wiltshire

CHAPTER I

DEATH AT
HIGH NOON

Mark Kennick was in the field, a quarter of a mile from the house, when the five riders rode into the courtyard. He had picked up the sound of their mounts a couple of minutes earlier and, for some reason he couldn't analyze, had pushed himself out of sight among the small stand of trees.

It was seldom they had any visitors and there was something about the riders that sent a little shiver of apprehension through him. There was a grim purpose in the way they dismounted and moved in a loose bunch towards the veranda. They all had the look of hired gunfighters about them, men intent on making trouble.

Over the past couple of years there had been reports of beef being rustled from several of the smaller ranches but since they had no cattle and were merely farmers, making their living from the land, they had been left alone. Gunfire occasionally erupted in the town but word was that Henders Rock was no worse than many of the frontier towns.

The last man to have paid his father a visit had been Seth Corby, perhaps the biggest landowner in this part of the territory. That had been two days earlier and he recalled how he had heard Corby and his father arguing angrily in the small front room while he had listened from the top of the stairs.

It had soon become evident that Corby had made a further offer to buy their land. From the sound of his father's raised voice it was clear this was an offer which his father had refused. He had often heard his parents say that Corby was a man intent on getting his hands on all of the land around Henders Rock and that which he couldn't buy at a quarter of its worth, he took by force.

Mark knew very little more about Corby but from what he had heard, he was not a man to cross. Once he set his mind on acquiring something, he got it. When the landowner had left, storming out of the house with his hard features twisted into a scowl of anger, Mark had tried to question his father but to no avail.

From the worried expression on his mother's face, however, he guessed that Corby had made threats against them and now, barely two days later, these five gunmen had arrived, clearly looking for trouble.

Slowly, taking care not to be seen, he edged his way forward through the trees. If only he had a gun, he might be able to do something, even though he had never used one in his life. His father had always insisted that there were to be no firearms in the house; that violence only served to breed further violence.

He could hear voices coming from inside with an occasional harsh laugh from one of the men. Then, without warning, two shots rang out. The unexpectedness of them jerked him stiffly upright. The next moment, his sister Amy appeared in the open doorway, a soundless scream on her face.

Stumbling down the steps, she reached the edge of the courtyard and started to run. One of the men came out of the door behind her. Grinning wolfishly, he lifted his Colt almost casually and fired a single shot which took Amy in the back. Throwing out her arms, she fell forward into the dust and lay still. Still smiling, the killer thrust the weapon back into its holster and moved towards the waiting horses.

Gritting his teeth in futile anger and anguish, Mark could only stand there, knowing there was nothing he could do. From what he had just seen, it was immediately obvious that his sister was dead.

One by one, the remaining four men came out. In the harsh sunlight, Mark saw their faces clearly. Each one imprinted itself on his brain and he knew he would remember them until the day he died.

One of the men, shorter than the others, but clearly the leader, paused with his hand on the bridle. 'You're sure that's all of 'em?' he called harshly. 'We don't want to leave any witnesses.'

'There's nobody left in the house, Jeth,' answered one of the others.

'All right. One of you check the stable yonder. Pedro, you go round the back. The boss won't be pleased if we leave anyone who could talk.'

Very slowly, Mark sank to his knees behind the tree, pressing himself hard against the trunk. He saw two of the men move away. One of them walked across the courtyard and pulled open the door of the stable. Holding his gun ready; he went inside, and reappeared a couple of minutes later shaking his head.

'Nobody in there,' he called harshly. 'Just one mount and a buckboard.'

The man called Pedro came riding back a moment later: 'Nobody around the back.' he said loudly. 'I reckon we got 'em all.'

Climbing into their saddles, the gunmen kicked spurs to their mounts' flanks and rode off in a cloud of white dust. Not until they had disappeared completely along the trail was Mark able to move. He felt numb as if all the feeling had been drained from him. Desperately, he tried to tell himself that all of this wasn't happening, that he had imagined it all.

Then, running forward, he went down on one knee beside his sister. Blood grew in a widening stain on her blue dress. Her eyes were wide open but they saw nothing. Gently, he turned her over and placed her on her back. A trickle of blood oozed from the corner of her mouth and he wiped it away with his sleeve.

For over a minute, he knelt there and then pushed himself upright. It was at that moment that he noticed the smoke. It came pouring out of the door and the open windows. The sharp crackle of flames reached him as he thrust himself forward.

As he reached the door, the searing heat came out to meet him. Inside, the room was an inferno. Already, the fire had already taken a firm hold. Flames were licking hungrily across the floor and along the walls. Through the tears which threatened to blind him, he saw his mother lying on the floor beside the table.

His father was slumped by the window, his shoulders against the wall. Choking as the smoke caught at his throat and went down into his lungs, he grasped his mother beneath the arms and somehow managed to pull her out onto the veranda, down into the courtyard. She had been shot through the chest.

Shielding his eyes with his arm, he dashed back inside. By now the smoke was so dense he could hardly make out anything. To one side, the flames had reached the ceiling, climbing up the drapes on either side of the windows. Almost blindly, he found his way to where his father lay. Bending, he took his father's weight across his shoulders. Staggering drunkenly from side to side, he fell against the table as he fought his way to the door. With an effort, he got outside and sank down onto the wooden planks of the veranda.

Great racking coughs tore at his throat as he wiped the tears from his eyes. The heat from the blazing house seared his back and shoulders. Reaching down, he felt his mother's wrist but there was no pulse. He realized she must have died instantly as the heavy calibre slug tore through her heart. Turning his attention to his father, he saw the other's eyes flick open and a low groan escaped from his throat.

'Just lie still, Pa,' he said hoarsely. 'You're goin' to make it. I'll ride into town and get the doctor.'

His father shook his head slowly. Swallowing thickly, he muttered, 'Not a chance, Mark. Your mother and sister, are they—?'

'They're both dead, Pa. Amy ran out and they shot her down like a dog in the courtyard.'

His father tried to speak again but it was several moments before he got the faltering words out. 'Listen, son. Corby's at the back o' this. I'm sure of it. He . . . he wants this land and . . . he'll kill to get it.'

'I'll stop him, Pa.' Mark felt like crying but the tears refused to come.

A moment later, his father's head fell back limply onto the wooden boards and a faint sigh came from his lips.

Standing beside the three bodies lying in the courtyard, Mark knew there was no chance of saving the house. The fire had taken too firm a hold. Now there was only one thought uppermost in his mind. It supplanted the grief and fury in his mind, leaving them to simmer just beneath the surface.

If Seth Corby had sent those hired killers to do this, to massacre unarmed folk, then he intended to kill him no matter how long it took. He recalled the individual faces of those five men and knew they were indelibly fixed in his mind. They would pay for this, all of them, if it was the last thing he ever did.

How long he stood there, with his shadow moving slowly around him as the sun dipped from its zenith, he couldn't tell. A little earlier, the roof of the house had fallen in and now there was only a thinning cloud of smoke and a few flickers of flame among the dying embers.

Bitterly, he knew that this was no place for him now. In the space of a few short minutes, he had lost everything. He could not stay here. There was, however, one last chore he had to do before he left. Going over to the stable, he brought out the stallion and hitched up the buckboard. Very carefully, he laid the bodies of his family into it and then led the horse out of the courtyard and into the field. At the very bottom, he stopped, taking up the shovel he had brought with him.

By the time he had dug the three graves, side by side, twilight had fallen. The first sky sentinels were beginning to show towards the east. Lowering the bodies into the ground, he wiped the sweat from his face, then shovelled the earth over them. He worked mechanically, without conscious thought, scarcely aware of his movements. Then, patting down the mounds with the shovel, he straightened.

Seated at his usual table in the corner of the Silver Star saloon, Seth Corby struck a sulphur match and waved it negligently over the end of his cigar. Three men were seated around the table with him. On his left was Jed Foran, the banker, small and stout, a man who always carried a derringer in his waistcoat pocket.

The two other men were both professional gamblers. Henri Devaroux and Hal Manson normally worked the large paddle steamers which plied the Mississippi from New Orleans. Only when things got too hot for them on the river and accusations of cheating were made against them did they move inland until things cooled down.

Already, Devaroux had a large pile of notes in front of him and Corby's temper had worsened as his own pile had dwindled. He had the feeling that it was more than just coincidence that he seemed to be getting bad cards but, with an effort, he kept his thoughts to himself. Both the slim, extravagantly dressed Frenchman facing him across the table and the other sitting on his right were known to have killed several men who had accused them of cheating.

Blowing a cloud of smoke in front of him, he scarcely glanced up as the saloon doors opened and Jeth Monaghan came in. The gunman walked over to the table and stood silently beside Corby for several moments, waiting patiently until the other threw in his hand with a snort of anger.

Turning his head, he stared up at Monaghan and took note of the expression on the other's swarthy features. Pushing back his chair, he got to his feet. 'If you would excuse me, gentlemen,' he said thinly. 'Some urgent business has just come up. Deal me out o' the next hand. I'll be back in a few moments.'

He followed Monaghan to the bar, choosing a place well away from anyone else so they could not be overheard. Not looking at the other, he said quietly, 'Well, everythin' go all right?' He studied the man's face in the mirror behind the bar, watching his expression closely.

'It was just like you said, Mr Corby. They never expected us. We shot all three and then fired the place. You shouldn't have any more trouble gettin' your hands on that land and filing the deeds.'

Corby turned his head sharply. 'Three of 'em?' he repeated, hissing the words savagely through his teeth.

'Why sure. Kennick, his wife and the girl. We searched the house and stable before torchin' the building. There was nobody else there.'

Corby sucked in a harsh breath. 'You goddamned fool. There were four in that family. You tellin' me the son is still alive?' For a moment, Corby seemed on the point of striking the other.

'We killed everyone who was there,' Monaghan muttered defensively. 'You never mentioned anythin' about a son. There was no sign of anyone else.'

'You say you searched the stable. Was there a mount there?'

'There was one and a buckboard. That was all.'

Corby stepped closer. Inwardly, he had hoped that perhaps Mark Kennick had taken the horse and buckboard and ridden into town. But now, everything pointed to him having been there and almost certainly witnessing everything. That raised more problems than Corby liked.

Through his teeth, he muttered, 'Then Kennick's son must've been somewhere around and possibly saw it all. You can be damned sure he saw your faces and if he should connect any of you with me, someone's

13

goin' to pay. I don't hire men who make mistakes.'

Quite suddenly, Monaghan recognized the precariousness of his position. He had seen the other shoot men down when they didn't do exactly what he told them.

Without any change of expression, Corby grated, 'I'm givin' you one last chance, Monaghan. You'll ride out right now, go back to the Kennick place and you don't come back into town unless you can tell me that Mark Kennick is dead. You understand?'

Monaghan nodded. 'I understand, Mr Corby.'

'See to it that you do. This time you'll go alone. I'll deal with the others later. Now get going.'

His eyes smouldering with suppressed anger, Seth Corby watched Monaghan go, then went back to rejoin the others at the card table.

There was still a faint haze of choking grey smoke hanging over the burnt-out ruins when Mark returned to the courtyard. There was something at the back of his mind but with all that had happened, it had gone. Then he remembered. He needed money if he was to purchase guns to avenge his parents and sister.

He knew his father kept money in an iron box in the bottom drawer of his desk. Whether it had survived the fire, he didn't know. Cautiously, he clambered over the remains of the veranda. There was little left of the desk. Bending, he sifted among the ashes where his father's papers were now nothing more than ash.

Pulling the still-hot embers aside, he caught a

glimpse of something which shone dully in the light. Bringing it out into the open, he recognized the box, still intact with the key in the lock. He took it outside, coughing as the smoke bit at the back of his throat. The key resisted stubbornly but eventually he succeeded in opening it.

He reckoned there was close to $200 there and fortunately the box had protected them from the fire and heat. At the bottom, he found the deeds to the ranch. Taking them out, he thrust them into his jacket pocket, tossing the empty box into the dirt.

His initial intention, after burying his family, had been to hitch up the buckboard and ride into town to inform the sheriff what had happened but then caution and common sense had taken over. If those killers had been working for Corby it would not be long before they knew he was still alive.

Riding into Henders Rock in darkness would be a fool thing to do. Almost all of the folk in town knew him. He doubted if any would point him out to strangers but Corby would certainly recognize him and that was a chance he didn't mean to take.

He decided to sleep in the stable. If any of those killers did come back looking for him, the horse would give him warning of it. After giving some feed to the stallion, he stretched himself out on the straw, leaving the door partially open.

More than once, he wished his father had not been so adamant about not keeping guns in the house. Without any weapon but his knife, he would stand little chance against armed killers. Rolling onto his side where he could just make out the gaunt ruins in the faint wash of moonlight, he closed his eyes.

The faint snicker of the horse, standing patiently close by in the darkness, woke him some time later. He came alert immediately, searching around him for what could have spooked the animal. Easing himself quietly to his feet, he moved to the door and peered out. Nothing moved in the long shadows.

Then, stiffening against the side of the stable, he caught a fragmentary glimpse of a dark figure that had appeared for a brief moment close to the fire-blackened wall in the near distance. The moonlight had glinted off the drawn Colt in the other's hand. Swiftly, Mark glanced around him.

There was no chance of getting out of the stable without being seen. If he tried that, he would be shot down before he could take half-a-dozen paces just as Amy had been.

Glancing up, he noticed the large ledge at the back of the stable, full of feed for the horse. Taking care to make no noise, he pulled himself up onto it. There was a large bale just in front of him and he crouched down behind it. A moment later, there was the sound of stealthy footsteps approaching the stable. A dark shadow fell across the narrow opening where the moonlight shone in.

Swiftly, he pulled his head down. Remaining absolutely still, he waited tensely. The man was evidently taking no chances. He stood just inside the doorway, evidently waiting until his eyes grew accustomed to the gloom, his Colt ready for any sudden movement.

Then the man spoke, his voice low and hard. 'If you're hidin' in here, Kennick, you'd better come out with your hands lifted where I can see 'em. Mister Corby just wants a word with you, that's all. Ain't nothin' going to happen if you do as I say.'

Mark kept his lips pressed tightly together. The man took a couple of steps forward until he was standing directly beneath where he was hidden. 'Your pa was a fool. He was made a good offer and that still stands. Reckon you could do with some money now there's nothin' left of the house. The land ain't worth much but Mr Corby's willin' to give you a good price for it.'

Knowing the other was deliberately taunting him into doing something rash, Mark waited then placed both hands hard against the side of the heavy bale. Exerting all of his strength, he thrust it forward. For a second, it teetered on the edge of the ledge.

Monaghan caught the sudden movement from the edge of his vision. Instinctively, he thrust himself to one side. The falling bale missed his head but caught him a glancing blow on the right shoulder knocking him sideways. Pain lanced agonizingly along Monaghan's arm as his finger jerked instinctively on the trigger of the Colt.

The sound of the shot was deafening inside the confined space. The bullet tore into the ground in front of him. The next moment, before he could move, the stallion, spooked by the noise, reared up onto its hind legs.

Monaghan uttered a loud cry as his foot, hooked against the bale, threw him off balance. He hit the ground a split second before the flailing hoofs came down upon him. Gingerly, Mark lowered himself down and stood staring at the prone body on the floor. He prodded it with his foot. The way the man flopped limply onto his back told Mark he was dead.

The hammering hoofs had crushed his ribs and smashed his spine. Bending, Mark instantly recognized the man as the leader of those five killers who had ridden in earlier. Calming down the frightened stallion, he pondered what to do next.

Inwardly, he felt certain this man had ridden out here alone. Had there been any others they would have come running up on hearing that shot. But it would not be long before the gunman was missed. When that happened, his position would become extremely precarious.

He could take the stallion, ride out, and keep on riding, possibly clear to the California border. But he had made a solemn promise to his father just before he had died. That was a promise he could not break.

For a moment he considered taking the guns this man wore; then rejected the idea at once. He could not use those weapons which had been responsible for killing his family.

Very slowly, he edged out into the courtyard, his gaze flicking from side to side as he searched keenly for any shadows that moved. There was only silence and stillness. Then a faint sound reached him from somewhere on the other side of the ruins. Crouching down, he moved cautiously along the charred remnant of the veranda.

He relaxed slightly as he saw the horse standing patiently a few yards away, the bridle looped over a tree branch.

CHAPTER II

AVENGING GUNS

The frontier town of Henders Rock simmered in the heat of early afternoon when Mark Kennick rode in, hot and hungry. He carried no guns and the horse he rode was now the only thing he had in the world; that, and the intense bitterness and seething hatred which now filled him to the core.

Reining up in front of the sheriff's office, he slid from the saddle and looped the reins over the rail, his boots kicking up little spurts of dust from the street. Stepping up onto the boardwalk, he pushed open the office door and went inside.

The office was empty but there was a half-smoked cigar in the ashtray on the desk.

'Sheriff McKinrick,' Mark called loudly.

A moment later there came the sound of a cell door being closed along the passage leading to the back of the building. McKinrick came in, closing the door behind him. He was a big man in his middle fifties, his dark hair greying a little at the temples. He stared at Mark in surprise.

'I was just takin' a nap in one o' the cells back there. It's a mite cooler than out here.' Noticing the expression on Mark's face, he added sharply, 'Somethin' wrong, Mark?'

Somehow, Mark got the words out. 'They're all dead, Sheriff. Pa, Ma and Amy – all three of 'em. Five killers just shot 'em down and then fired the place. I—'

Stepping forward, a serious expression on his weather-beaten face, McKinrick took the other's arm and led him to the chair in front of the desk. 'Sit down, Mark. Tell me all that happened. You say some gang rode out to your place and killed your family?'

Going back to his seat, the sheriff opened one of the drawers and took out a bottle and glass. Pouring out some of the whiskey, he pushed the glass across the desk. 'Here, drink this. It might help a little.'

He waited as Mark took several swallows of the liquor, grimacing as the raw spirit hit the back of his throat. He could tell that the young man facing him was still in shock and waited patiently until the other had finished the drink. Then he said quietly, 'Just when did this happen?'

Swallowing with an effort, Mark hesitated; then said hoarsely, 'Yesterday afternoon. I was out in the field when I heard these riders comin'. Like I said, there were five of 'em and at first I thought they might be drifters lookin' for jobs. I was among the trees at the time and I guess they didn't see me.'

He shifted uncomfortably in the chair, staring

21

down at the glass in his hand. With an obvious effort, he lifted his head to look squarely at the lawman. 'I saw them go inside and I could just hear my pa. He was shoutin' and sounded angry. Then . . . then there were two shots.

'I wanted to run in to see what had happened but I couldn't. I knew there was nothin' I could do. As you know, Pa would never have a gun in the house, always said that violence breeds violence. Then Amy came runnin' out. She'd only run a couple o' steps when this gunman came to the door and shot her in the back.'

McKinrick placed the tips of his fingers together, his face set into a grim expression. There was a stunned expression on his lined features. 'I knew your pa well.' he said slowly. 'He was a good friend o' mine, a peaceable man. But since he turned down Seth Corby's first offer to buy him out, I told him time and time again to get a gun, even just to protect himself. But he wouldn't listen.'

'It wouldn't have helped.' Anger and bitterness showed through the anguished look on Mark's face. 'Not against those hired killers. Corby knew that when he sent those men. They knew no one in the house was armed yet they just shot 'em.'

McKinrick pushed back his chair and stood up, looking down at the other. 'Let me give you some good advice, son. How old are you now – twenty-four? – and you've never had a gun in your hand. Don't go around Henders Rock makin' accusations against Seth Corby. He's a mighty influential man in town and unless you've got some proof that would stand up in front of a jury, you'd better keep those thoughts to yourself.'

'Proof!' Mark's lips thinned down across his teeth. 'What more proof do you need? There was nothin' in the house worth stealin'. Those killers didn't come to rob us: somebody sent 'em, Sheriff. I buried the only family I had in the ground at the bottom o' the field, and someone is goin' to pay for this. One of the gang came back durin' the night and tried to kill me.'

'You saw him?'

Mark nodded. 'He had me cornered in the stable. I dropped a hay bale on him and when his gun went off it spooked the horse. The stallion killed him when he fell.'

'Goddamn. You know who this man was?'

'I recognized him as the leader of the gang. One o' the others called him Jeth.'

McKinrick pursed his lips. 'Can't say I've heard the name. If he and those others are working for Corby, I sure ain't seen anyone like them around town. He'll have brought them in from across the border and you'll never be able to prove a goddamn thing.'

Leaning forward, resting his weight on his hands, the sheriff thrust his face close up to Mark's. 'Listen to me – and listen good, Mark. I'm tellin' you this for your own sake. You've just lost your whole family and I sympathize with that. But you've got to think calmly and clearly. Go up against Corby and you'll be dead by this time tomorrow. In fact the best advice I can give you is leave town.

'I'm not sayin' Corby is behind this but if he is, he'll know damned well he can't get his hands on the deeds to that land as long as you're alive. He wants you dead, Mark. You're no gunslinger. You've never owned a gun in your life let alone fired one.'

'Then by God, I'll get one.' Mark stood up so quickly, the chair fell over. He made no effort to pick it up.

McKinrick straightened, sighed, and spread his hands in resignation. 'So you get yourself a gun. That'll be easy enough – but what then? You'll never make a Billy the Kid and—' He closed his mouth with a snap. The office door had closed and he was talking to himself.

After eating a meal in the small cantina a little way along the street, Mark made his way to the hardware store next to the stables. Ed Clayton, the storekeeper eyed him with a look of mild curiosity. 'You in town lookin' for some tools, Mark?' he inquired. 'Your pa was in last week askin' about a saw and I—'

'We won't be needin' any more tools, Ed,' Mark said thinly. 'I just need a couple o' guns, a belt, and some shells.'

The storekeeper's expression turned to one of astonishment. Finally, he said, 'You want some guns? I've known your father all my life and I know he's always been against the use o' guns. Now you walk into my store askin' for guns. Why would you—?'

'My father's dead,' Mark said thinly. 'Him, my mother and sister – shot down by a band o' gunhawks. I've just buried the three of 'em.'

'Hellfire. I'm mighty sorry to hear that, Mark.' Clayton said. 'You know who did this?'

'Sure. A bunch o' gunslingers hired by Corby. He tried to buy our spread and when Pa wouldn't sell out to him, he had them all killed.' Mark almost choked on the bitterness that welled through him. 'Now, will you let me have those guns?'

The other stared hard at him for a long moment, noticing the look in Mark's eyes and the grim set of his jaw, which etched his features with shadows. Then he shrugged and went to the rear of the store. Coming back, he laid a gunbelt and twin Colts on the counter. 'These are the best I've got,' he said. Reluctantly, he pushed them towards Mark. 'I only hope you know what you're doin'.'

Taking the gunbelt, Mark buckled it around his waist. It felt heavy and awkward and he had the sudden feeling that, by this simple act, he had done something which was to change his life completely. Clayton watched him from beneath lowered brows. For a moment, he seemed on the point of saying something; then bit it back.

'I'll need a couple o' boxes of shells.'

Bringing them from the shelf behind him, the other said, 'Why not let the law take care o' these killers, Mark? Sheriff McKinrick is a straight-shooter. If Seth Corby is at the back o' this, he'll bring him in for trial. Do you reckon you could identify those killers if you saw any of 'em again?'

'I saw all five of 'em. They didn't bother to hide their faces. Whoever sent 'em, he'd have told them there was nobody out there who could give 'em any trouble. As for the law, this is somethin' I have to do myself.' Glancing up from thrusting the cartridges into the gunbelt after filling the chambers of the Colts, he went on, 'You seen anythin' of five strangers around town in the last couple o' days?'

The other shook his head. 'Nope. Can't say I have. But then I'm in the store all day. I don't see much o' what goes on outside in the street.' Glancing down at the Colts, he went on, 'That'd usually be seventy-five dollars but since it's you, I'll let you have the lot for fifty.'

'Thanks.' Mark laid the money on the counter.

As he reached the door, Clayton called. 'I know just how you feel, Mark. But getting yourself shot won't solve anythin' and it sure won't avenge the killin' of your family. Apart from those rattlers who killed them, there are plenty o' gunslingers in this town who'll recognize a greenhorn when they see one and put a bullet in you before you can draw those guns.'

'So I should just forget all that's happened. Is that what you're tellin' me?'

The other came from around the counter and laid a hand on Mark's arm. 'No, you shouldn't just forget. All I'm sayin' is don't go after these killers like a demented steer. That way you'll be a candidate for Boot Hill before dark. Keep out o' sight for a while. If you're intent on goin' after Corby and these men, learn how to handle those Colts.'

Mark knew there was sense in what Clayton was saying. Standing in the doorway, he forced some of the anger and bitterness from his mind. As the store-keeper had said, he had to act with a clear head or he would end up on the floor of a saloon with a bullet in his chest.

As if sensing the indecision in him, the other went on quietly, but firmly. 'I guess there's nowhere for you to go back to, Mark. If you ain't intent on ridin' out, I can put you up for a while, upstairs over the store. Nobody will think o' lookin' there.'

'All right.' Mark gave a sullen nod. 'I'll stay for a couple o' days but I'll be keepin' watch for those other four killers – and for Seth Corby.'

'Now you're talkin' sense.' Clayton turned and led the way back into the store. There was a flight of stairs at the rear of the counter and he went up them ahead of Mark. Opening a door at the end of a short passage, he stood on one side to allow Mark to enter.

Pointing, Clayton said, 'You can keep a watch on the town from the window yonder. None of your friends will talk but Corby knows you well. Just keep out o' sight. I'll bring you some grub.'

At the Triple X ranch, Seth Corby paced slowly up and down the big room overlooking the courtyard. Watching him in silence, Pedro Dominguez lounged in the chair at the side of the large mahogany table. The Mexican knew better than to speak. Whenever the rancher was in this mood, he could vent his anger on anyone.

Finally, Corby stopped his pacing and stood with his hands clasped tightly behind his back, glaring through the window. Without turning, he said roughly, 'Have you got any idea why Monaghan didn't come back last night from the Kennick place?'

'None at all, Señor Corby. If, as you say, those

people never carried guns, it should have been a simple matter for Jeth to kill Kennick's son if he was still there.'

'Maybe Mark Kennick wasn't there and Monaghan's too scared to come back to face me. Could be he's ridden out.'

'That is not the way Jeth operates, *señor*,' Pedro replied smoothly.

'Then why the hell isn't he here?' There was a venomous anger in the rancher's voice as a new idea came into his mind. He spun on his heel. 'Unless he's tryin' to double-cross me. If he's killed Kennick and found those deeds—' He left the rest of his sentence unsaid.

'Perhaps we should ride out and see for ourselves,' the Mexican suggested.

Corby chewed on that for a moment, then gave a terse nod. 'Saddle up the buckboard.' he ordered thinly. 'If Monaghan has any ideas of claimin' that land for himself, I'll see him in Hell first.'

Five minutes later, his mind still seething with speculation, Corby drove the buckboard out of Henders Rock with Dominguez riding beside him. What had earlier seemed to be a simple way of getting his hands on that land had now become a big problem. Had the five gunmen he'd brought in from across the Mexican border carried out his orders efficiently, those deeds would have been in his hands by now.

The lawyer, Simmins, would have transferred the title to him and that would have been the end of the matter. Now, with Mark Kennick still alive somewhere and Monaghan not showing up, things were beginning to get out of hand.

Half an hour later they came within sight of the Kennick spread. Seated on the buckboard, Corby surveyed the smoke-blackened ruins of the house. There was no sign of any bodies and the suspicion that Mark Kennick had been somewhere close by, had witnessed all that had happened, and later buried his family someplace, now crystallized into certainty. Stepping down, he walked across the courtyard towards the ruins and it was then he noticed the strongbox lying in the dust near the steps.

Bending, he picked it up and threw back the lid. It was empty. Tossing it away in his anger, he snarled to Pedro, 'That is where the deeds to this place would have been kept. Someone has taken them and if it wasn't Kennick's son, it must have been Monaghan.'

Nodding in agreement; Pedro said smoothly; 'There was a stallion and a buckboard in the stable yonder when we came. I don't see any sign of either now.'

'Take a look in the stable,' Corby ordered. It was unlikely they would find anything here but things were not going the way he wanted and if Mark Kennick was still alive and in possession of those deeds he could make a lot of trouble.

A sudden shout from the stable jerked his head around sharply. Pedro called harshly, 'You'd better take a look in here, Señor Corby.'

Corby hurried over to the stable door. Brushing brusquely past the Mexican, Corby stepped inside. He immediately saw the body lying on the floor just inside the door.

'It's Monaghan,' Pedro said tautly.

'I can see that.' Corby snapped. Bending, he turned the crushed body over; then lifted his head to stare at Dominguez. His first intuitive thought was that the man had been shot, that somehow Mark Kennick had got himself a gun and taken Monaghan unawares. Now he saw that he was mistaken. Monaghan's chest had been crushed.

Picking up the Colt lying close to the body, he checked the chambers. 'One shot has been fired,' he said tonelessly. 'It must have frightened the horse.' He glanced at the bale of hay, then kicked it aside with a swipe of his foot and examined the floor closely. 'There's no sign of blood anywhere. That means that if Kennick was in here, the slug from Jeth's gun missed its mark.'

'So this *hombre* Kennick must still be somewhere around,' Dominguez put in.

Corby straightened up and thrust the Colt into his belt. 'Seems like that to me,' he agreed tightly. 'And he's taken the stallion but not the buckboard. The question is: has he decided to ride out for good – or is he still in town somewhere?'

Rubbing a hand over his stubbled chin, Pedro remarked, 'Reckon if he did ride into town, he'd make for the sheriff. Perhaps McKinrick could tell us something.'

Going outside, Corby said harshly, 'I'll arrange for somebody to come out here for Monaghan. First I want a word with McKinrick.'

The sheriff was seated outside his office, waving

his hat across his face when Corby rode in, stopping the buckboard with a savage jerk on the reins. McKinrick could tell from the expression on the landowner's broad features that there was trouble brewing.

Stepping up onto the boardwalk, Corby said sharply, 'I want a word with you, Sheriff.'

Placing his hat back on his head, McKinrick said coolly, 'What have you got on your mind, Corby?'

'I've just ridden back from the Kennick spread. There's a dead man there in the stable and the house has been burned to the ground. Weren't any sign o' the family. Do you know anything o' what happened?'

Taking a half-smoked cigar from his shirt pocket, McKinrick thrust it between his lips. Striking a sulphur match, he applied it to the end. Speaking around it, he said tautly, 'I've heard that a bunch o' polecats rode out there yesterday and killed that family in cold blood.' He met Corby's stare directly. 'Reckon I could ask you and your friend here if you know anything about it.'

Corby's face hardened into a mask of suppressed anger. 'Don't fool around with me, McKinrick. It was my say-so that put you in office and I can just as easily get you out.'

The sheriff eased himself out of his chair. 'While I'm still the law in Henders Rock, I intend to do my job as I see fit. Pretty soon, everyone in town is goin' to know that somebody sent a bunch o' killers out there to that spread with orders to murder everyone they found and I intend to find out who it was and

31

see they're tried and strung up from the nearest tree.'

Through his teeth, Corby rasped, 'If you're inferrin' that I, or any of my men, had anythin' to do with it, you're ridin' a dangerous trail, McKinrick.'

'Maybe so. But it seems to me that you're the only one with a reason for wantin' the Kennicks out o' the way.'

Corby's face whitened under the implied accusation. Then he pulled himself under tight control. In a more conciliatory tone, he went on, 'It's common knowledge I asked Kennick to sell that land and I offered him a fair price. I rode out there to make him a better, and final, offer. Instead, I found the place burned down and no sign of Kennick or his family. All I'm askin' is what happened and if there were any survivors so I can put my offer to them.'

The lawman's lips twisted into a wry grin. 'Mark's still alive if that's what you want to know.'

Corby's eyes narrowed to slits. 'You got any idea where he is? That place is no good to him now and he might be a little more amenable to my offer.'

'Somehow I doubt that. All he said was he's goin' to get himself a gun and then he's ridin' out. But my guess is he'll be back someday and he'll hunt down the men who did this.'

Corby threw a quick glance in Pedro's direction. Stepping down from the boardwalk he climbed back into the buckboard. To McKinrick he said harshly, 'If you should see the young fool, you'd better warn him off. I don't take too kindly to folk makin' these accusations against me.'

Angrily, he slashed the whip across the horse's flanks and sent it racing along the dusty street. Stopping outside the hardware store, he went inside. Clayton glanced up quickly from behind the counter. Seeing who it was, he kept his face expressionless.

'You sell any guns today?' he demanded brusquely.

For a moment, Clayton hesitated, then nodded. 'Happen I did, Mr Corby.'

'Mind tellin' me who bought them?'

'It was young Kennick. Said his family had all been killed and he meant to get whoever had done it.'

'So he's still in town.'

'Not if he's taken my advice,' Clayton remarked evenly.

'Oh.' A strange glint came into the landowner's eyes. 'What was that?'

The other shrugged. 'Mark Kennick ain't ever handled a gun in his life. I told him if he wanted to avenge his family he should ride out o' town and learn how to handle those Colts before he found himself up in Boot Hill.'

'You think he'll take your advice?'

'Reckon so,' Clayton answered. 'Leastways, he took the north trail out o' town. Didn't say where he was headed. My guess is he's halfway to the border by now.'

Corby considered that for a moment, then turned on his heels and left. Clayton waited until the rancher had turned the buckboard, heading back into town before going up the creaking stairs. He found Mark standing by the window.

'I told him you'd left town, Mark,' Clayton said

softly. 'From the way he acted, I'm danged sure he sent those men out to your spread. He won't rest now until you're dead and he's got his hands on those deeds.'

'Then I guess it's up to me to see that he never does. One day I'm goin' to kill Seth Corby and anyone who sides with him.' There was a note of grim determination in Mark's tone which made Clayton flinch and draw back a little.

Shaking his head a little, he said thinly, 'Reckon you'll have to learn to handle those Colts before you do that, son. Take my advice. Ride out o' Henders Rock as soon as you get the chance. That way you might stay alive long enough to avenge your family.'

Mark thought that over and then nodded. The anger and bitterness were still there inside him but he knew that if he gave in to these emotions he was as good as dead. Now was the time for clear, rational thinking.

'I'll get you some grub,' Clayton said making his way to the stairs.

When the storekeeper had gone, Mark turned his attention back to the street outside. He didn't doubt that Corby would never stop looking for him. But if the rancher had any sense he would keep those four remaining killers out of town for the time being, knowing that if he, Mark, was still in town, he would recognize them immediately and get word to the sheriff. He had the feeling that Corby didn't want him killed in the open.

The townsfolk would be well aware of his father's aversion to guns of any kind and if he was shot by one of Corby's men, they would immediately pin the wholesale murder of an unarmed family on him. At the moment, Corby would do all he could to distance himself from what had happened at the spread.

From the window, he noticed the saloon directly opposite the hardware store. A small bunch of riders came along the street, stopping outside. He studied them closely as they dismounted and went inside. None of them were the men he had seen at the spread the previous day but he guessed they were all Corby's hired hands.

Ten minutes later, Clayton came back with a plate of bacon, eggs and beans together with a mug of steaming coffee. Placing them on the small table, the storekeeper said gruffly. 'If you are figurin' on ridin' out, Mark, I suggest you wait until after dark. I've tethered your mount at the back o' the store. Nobody'll think o' looking there.'

'Thanks, Ed.' Seating himself at the table, he ate ravenously, realizing that it was the first meal he had eaten for more than twenty-four hours.

CHAPTER III

CHANCE MEETING

Henders Rock was its normal busy and boisterous place that evening as Mark slipped out of the back door of the hardware store. His mount was still there tethered to a short rail. Feeling in the saddle pouch, his fingers came into contact with the metal box containing the money and deeds.

Clayton had accompanied him to the door. Standing in the shadows, the storekeeper murmured softly, 'Better take the back street yonder, Mark. There are plenty of folk around in town this time o' night.'

Mark hesitated, then shook his head. 'First I've got to ask a few questions, get some names.'

'How the hell do you figure on doin' that?' Clayton demanded.

'There's only one place I can get any information – across the street in the saloon. I've been watchin' the place all evening and none o' those critters who murdered my family have gone inside. I know the bartender. Reckon he'll tell me what I want to know. Then I'll ride out.'

'Don't be a goddamned fool, Mark. Some o' those men in there are a mite too handy with their guns. Don't forget, there are a few folk in town who didn't get on too well with your father. If they see you in there wearin' a gunbelt there's no tellin' what they'll do.'

'Reckon I'll just have to take that chance,' Mark replied shortly.

Clayton spread his hand in a resigned gesture. 'Why throw your life away? Nobody in the saloon can tell you anythin' you don't already know.'

'Maybe not.' Mark was adamant. 'But somebody knows somethin'. I aim to know who my enemies are and who I can trust.'

'Then on your own head be it,' he muttered harshly. 'I've done all I can do to make you see some sense.' Turning on his heel he went back inside, closing the door softly behind him.

Leading the horse to the end of the alley, Mark paused and threw a swift, appraising glance along the street in both directions. There were several people on the boardwalks, mostly townsfolk taking advantage of the cooler air after the scorching heat of the day. Slowly, he crossed the street to where several horses were tethered to the rail fronting the saloon. Looping the reins over the rail, he hitched the heavy gunbelt higher about his waist and stepped up onto the wooden slats.

Pushing open the door, he went inside. Most of

the tables were already occupied. A handful of men were stood at the bar on the far side, their backs to him. On the small stage in the far corner, a young woman was singing to the accompaniment of a tinny piano. She had a pleasant, husky voice but it was clear that very few of the customers were listening to her.

Going over to the bar, he picked a spot well away from the others and waited until the barkeep sidled up to him.

Seeing him, a look of surprise flashed across the other's fleshy features. Leaning forward, he said in a low voice, 'What the hell are you doin' in here, Mark?' He suddenly noticed the Colts, and went on, 'I heard about what happened at the spread and I sure am sorry. Your family was well liked in town. But you ain't figurin' on causin' any trouble in here, are you?'

'All I want is a drink and some information, Walt,' Mark said softly. 'Then I'll leave.'

Bringing over a bottle and glass, the other whispered, 'What kind of information?'

Pouring some of the whiskey into the glass, Mark said, 'There were five killers in that bunch which murdered my family. They must have known there were no guns in the house, that we couldn't defend ourselves, so they didn't bother to hide their faces.'

'You saw them?' The bartender's expression of surprise turned into one of apprehension.

Mark nodded, sipping the whiskey. 'I saw all five of 'em. I'd know them anywhere. One of 'em is dead. The horse trampled him when he tried to kill me in the stable last night. I'm plumb certain they were workin' for Seth Corby.'

Laying a hand on Mark's arm, the barkeep hissed urgently, 'Don't try to go up against Corby, Mark, even if you've got any proof it was him. The whole town knows he's broken the law on several occasions but even the law seems to be unable to do anythin' about it. You're no gunslinger. I'll wager you've never fired a gun in your life. Corby's gunhawks will kill you before you could touch those guns.'

'All I want you to tell me is whether you've seen five strangers in town over the past few days. One of 'em is a Mexican named Pedro.'

The bartender's forehead creased in concentration, his glance roving over the tables behind Mark. 'Most o' Corby's ranch-hands come into the saloon nearly every night but I can't say I've noticed any strangers among 'em. Certainly I've never seen anyone resembling this Pedro. Could be they've just ridden in from across the border.'

Mark finished his drink and set the glass down on the counter. As he did so, his glance fell on the long mirror at the back. Two men had scraped back their chairs and were staring in his direction. Then one of them said viciously, 'You at the bar, mister. Turn round.'

Very slowly, Mark turned, keeping his hands well away from his sides. He didn't recognize either of the two men but guessed they worked for Seth Corby.

'There's no call for any trouble, Jed,' called the bartender loudly. His right hand moved towards the shotgun just beneath the counter. 'The same goes for you too, Ben. This young fella is only here for a drink.'

Jed's right hand dropped towards the handle of his Colt. 'Keep your hands on the bar, Walt. Make a try for that scattergun you've got under the counter and it'll be the last thing you do.'

'Seems to us he was havin' quite a conversation with you,' Ben shouted loudly. 'Couldn't be he was askin' questions about Mr Corby, could it?'

'We was just talkin' about how his family was murdered yesterday by a gang o' hired killers,' Walt replied. He moved a little further from the counter.

'And he's spreadin' it around that Corby had somethin' to do with it. Is that the way of it?' There was a brief pause then, with a sneering grin, the other went on, 'I see he's wearin' guns. Let's see if he's got the guts to use 'em.'

'I don't want any trouble with either of you,' Mark said, forcing evenness into his voice. 'And I don't intend to draw on you.'

'Well now,' Jed sneered. 'you got the look of a farmer boy to me. This is a cattle town. We don't aim to have any earthbreakers movin' in, do we boys?' He glanced round at the rest of the men sitting nearby. 'If you ain't lookin' for trouble, why are you wearin' those guns?'

Mark remained silent. Inwardly, he knew his position was extremely precarious. These men were looking for trouble and he knew he didn't have a chance against them. Both were obviously seasoned gunfighters, possibly killers wanted by the law in half-a-dozen states. But so long as they worked for Corby, they were safe.

'You don't seem so keen to talk now,' Ben grunted. He deliberately moved a few feet from his companion, then advanced slowly in Mark's direction. 'Guess we'd better work you over before we run you out o' town, just to teach you to answer when you're spoken to.'

Mark turned back to the counter and picked up the whiskey bottle. The next moment several things happened so quickly that he could scarcely take them in. Ben's hand dropped swiftly, jerking his Colt from its holster, lining it up on Mark's back. Scarcely had the gun cleared leather than a single shot rang out.

Whirling quickly, Mark was just in time to see the Colt slip from the gunhawk's fingers and drop to the floor. Swaying on his feet, Ben remained upright for a few seconds, a look of amazed surprise on his face. Then he fell sideways, crashing against the nearby table.

His companion had already pulled his gun but it was not aimed at Mark. In the corner of the room a tall, hawk-faced man stood with two Colts balanced in his hands. One covered Jed. The other moved in a short arc across the rest of the men at the tables.

Grimly, with a note of iron in his tone, he said, 'Drop that gun, mister, or you get the same as your friend.'

The gunman hesitated for a moment; then let the gun clatter to the floor at his feet, his bearded features twisted into a mask of fury.

Turning slowly, the stranger said thinly, 'Everyone

41

else keep their hands where I can see 'em.' Glancing in Mark's direction, he went on thinly, 'Get out while you can. Fork your bronc and head north.'

Moving swiftly to the door, Mark went outside and climbed quickly into the saddle. Kicking spurs to the stallion's flanks he sent it running swiftly along the street. Glancing back he saw the stranger emerging from the saloon. The other swung himself onto the back of one of the horses and raced after Mark. Harsh, confused shouting erupted as a fusillade of shots followed them.

Then they were clear of the town, giving their mounts their heads as they took the narrow trail leading towards the hills. A few moments later, the stranger was riding beside him, his features a dim blur beneath the wide hat. Leaning sideways, the man called, 'Follow me. I don't reckon they'll come after us but it ain't wise to take chances.'

Forging a few yards ahead, the tall, thin man kept with the trail for half a mile, then abruptly swung his mount to the right. Without hesitation, Mark did likewise. A dense stand of trees bordered the trail at this point but somehow, his companion thrust his mount through the thick undergrowth.

Leafy branches slashed Mark's face as he tried to keep the other in sight. As he followed the dark figure, he wondered just who this stranger was, why he had intervened in the saloon, and why he seemed so certain they would not be followed.

Thinking back, he realized there had been something familiar about the other's face when he had seen it clearly in the lights of the saloon. Somewhere, he thought, he had seen this man before.

Ten minutes later, they entered a small clearing at one side of which was a small trapper's hut. Reining up in front of it, the other slipped from the saddle and motioned Mark to do likewise. 'We can stay here for the night but tomorrow we'll have to be out of the territory.'

'Won't those men from town find us here?' Mark asked.

The other shook his head and led the way inside. 'Like I said, I doubt if they'll come after us. If they're Corby's men they'll wait for his orders and my guess is he'll get the sheriff to form a posse. Since McKinrick is no particular friend o' Corby's I doubt if he'll do anything tonight. If he does, I'll get word of it.'

Lighting a lantern, the other placed it on the long wooden table. In the yellow glow, Mark studied him closely. He was an old man, he reckoned, well into his sixties. His face was wrinkled, the leathery flesh drawn tight against the cheek bones. But his eyes, a piercing blue, were vital and alive.

'The name's Mark Kennick,' Mark said. 'I want to thank you for what you did back there. If it hadn't been for you, I'd—'

'You have ended up on that saloon floor with a slug in your chest like that gunslinger.' The other regarded Mark solemnly for a moment, then said, 'You don't know who I am, do you?'

Mark shook his head. 'Your face is strangely familiar but I'm sure we've never met. When you stepped in back there I figured you for some kind o' lawman

43

– a federal marshal.'

The other uttered a harsh laugh. 'I ain't no marshal, young fella. The name's Frank Calhoun. You'll have seen my picture on a wanted poster in McKinrick's office. Oh, it's there all right – and in a dozen other sheriffs' offices. But right now there are four bounty hunters hopin' to claim a two thousand dollar reward for me, dead or alive.'

'Then why did you butt in? What difference was it to you if they killed me or not?'

'I could tell by the way you carry that gunbelt you don't know the first thing about guns. Those two men were seasoned killers. They recognized you're a greenhorn just as I did. I guess you've got a pretty good reason for wearing 'em but unless you learn how to handle a Colt you'll be dead in a couple o' days.'

'Then will you teach me how to use 'em?'

Calhoun made no reply. If he was surprised by the question, he gave no outward sign of it. Going to a small cupboard he took out some meat and a hand-ful of beans, throwing them into a pan. Ten minutes later he had a fire going and placed the pan over it. Bringing a couple of plates out, he set them on the table.

Only then did he speak. 'I'm a wanted outlaw, Mark. Taggin' along with me would bring you more trouble than you know. It ain't the law I'm bothered about. These frontier towns are full o' killers and outlaws and the law does nothin'. But those bounty hunters have got greed on their side and they'll never give up lookin' for me.'

'You saved my life. Teach me how to handle these guns and I'll help you if they do catch up with you.'

Calhoun regarded him with a shrewd glint in his eyes. Spooning the hot food onto the plates, he said, 'Get that grub down you. Then tell me what's ridin' you so hard. It must be somethin' mighty important.'

Between mouthfuls, Mark explained what had happened. Calhoun listened attentively without interrupting. When he had finished, the outlaw rolled a cigarette, lit it, and blew the smoke towards the ceiling, his lips pursed into a hard line. Through the smoke, he said tautly, 'So you're out for revenge on these *hombres* who killed your family. Guess I can understand that. And you believe this man Corby was at the back of it?'

'I'm sure,' Mark replied earnestly. 'He tried to get his hands on the land before but my father always refused to sell. Now he knows I'm still alive and I have the deeds he won't stop until I'm dead.'

Calhoun pondered on that for a moment; then nodded. 'All right. I'll teach you all I know but it'll take time and we can't stay here. Those four killers are already headed for Henders Rock.'

Mark glanced up from his plate. 'How do you know that?' he inquired.

Calhoun gave a wry smile. 'I make it my business to know these things. That's how I've stayed alive for so long.'

Seeing the expression of puzzlement on Mark's face, he went on, 'There's someone in town keepin' watch for me. Once those bounty hunters ride in, I'll know. Then it'll be time to move out.'

Getting to his feet, he pointed towards the far end of the room. 'There's a bunk yonder. You can use it for the night.'

'But won't you—' Mark began.

Calhoun shook his head. 'When you get to my age, you don't need much sleep. I'll keep watch on the trail yonder just in case any o' Corby's men decide to avenge the death o' one of their own.'

Mark accepted the offer gratefully, throwing himself down on the bunk and pulling the thick woollen cover over himself. The hut was warm and the last thing he saw before falling asleep was the old man tossing more wood onto the blazing fire.

When he woke the next morning he found Calhoun standing in the open doorway staring out into the brightening dawn. Swinging his legs to the floor, he straightened up and went to join him.

'Somethin' wrong?' Mark asked in a low whisper.

'There's a rider comin' along the trail from town,' Calhoun replied equally softly. He eased one of the Colts from its holster.

Mark listened intently. Within moments he picked out the steady approach of hoofbeats on the trail. As the other had said, there seemed to be only one man. The sound stopped and then they heard the snap of branches.

'Whoever they are, they're coming this way,' he hissed. 'It can't be the sheriff, he'd bring a posse with him and Corby wouldn't dare to come alone.'

A moment later, a low whistle sounded among the trees. Calhoun thrust his Colt back into its holster and stepped forward as the rider emerged from the trees, head bent low to avoid the thick, overhanging branches.

The rider reined up a couple of yards away and swung lithely from the saddle. Mark stared in sudden surprise. The rising sun glinted off rich chestnut hair. Mark guessed she was perhaps a couple of years younger than himself and she was the singer he had seen in the saloon the previous evening. But what was a woman doing here in cahoots with a wanted outlaw?

'Were you followed, Della?' Calhoun asked as she came towards them.

The girl shook her head emphatically, glancing at Mark with a look of curiosity and slight suspicion. 'No one followed me,' she said confidently. 'But who's this? I didn't expect to find anyone else here.'

'This is Mark Kennick. He—'

'You're the one whose family was murdered by gunslingers. I heard about that in town. But what are you doing here? I expected you'd be miles away by now, clear across the border. Corby has made the sheriff put out a wanted notice for you, reckons you killed one of his men last night in the saloon, that you shot him in the back as he was leaving.'

Turning to Mark, Calhoun said, 'I guess it's like you said – Corby must want you dead and he'll spin any lies to have you killed.'

'Did you shoot that man in the back?' Della demanded. Mark could see she was still suspicious of him.

Before he could answer, Calhoun said, 'No, Della,

47

he didn't. I shot that coyote when he tried to get Mark to go for his gun.' Turning to Mark, he went on, 'Della is my granddaughter. She's the one who keeps me informed as to the whereabouts of those bounty hunters.'

'That's why I came,' Della put in swiftly. 'They rode into town early this morning before first light and put up at the hotel after waking the sheriff. I guess they were questioning him about you. You'll have to leave right away, Grandfather. It won't take them long to pick up your trail here.'

'I'll go with you,' Mark said. 'You made a promise last night and I intend to hold you to it.'

'What kind of promise?' Della asked harshly. 'I guess by now you know who my grandfather is, an outlaw.'

Mark nodded. 'I know. I also know he saved my life and gave his word he'll teach me how to use these.' He gestured towards the Colts at his waist.

'You intend to turn him into an outlaw?' There was a note of accusation in the girl's tone as she faced her grandfather.

'Not an outlaw, Della,' the other admonished. 'But I figure a man has a right to avenge the murder of his family and if it takes guns to do that, then so be it.'

Without another word, Calhoun entered the hut and began getting his provisions together, packing his saddle-bags and thrusting a Winchester into the leather scabbard.

Five minutes later, they were ready. Swinging into the saddle, Mark threw a quick glance at Della. 'Are you ridin' back into town?' he asked.

She shook her head. 'I'm riding with you. I can handle a gun and things are getting a little hot in town. Some of the customers suspect who I really am.'

Mark swung on Calhoun. 'Surely you're not goin' to let her come with us. If those bounty hunters catch up with us—'

Calhoun shook his head: 'It's no use trying to stop her. She's as bull-headed as her mother.'

'But—'

'This is no time for arguments,' Della said, holding her head high. She climbed easily into the saddle. 'We have to put as many miles between Henders Rock and ourselves before those killers decide to come and take matters into their own hands.'

High noon found them in a deep canyon with sheer walls of red sandstone rising several hundred feet on both sides. Here there was some shade from the scorching midday sun but there was little to mitigate the blistering heat that poured down on them from the cloudless heavens.

They had ridden hard since leaving the small shack, occasionally glancing over their shoulders to check the trail at their backs. But there had been nothing, no dust clouds to indicate the presence of men riding swiftly.

Lifting himself a little in the saddle, Calhoun pointed almost directly ahead. 'There's an old Indian trail yonder at the far end of the canyon. Reckon there ain't many who know about it. We can rest the horses there and also watch the trail for any pursuit.'

Mark wiped the sweat from his face before nodding in silent agreement. He threw a swift glance at Della riding beside him. She gave him a faint smile but said nothing. Urging their mounts forward, they finally put them to the steep upgrade that marked the end of the ravine.

At the top, Calhoun reined up. He jerked his head to the left. 'You see the trail, Mark?' he asked, moistening his dust-caked lips.

Carefully, Mark scanned the region. About fifty yards away was a dense stretch of mesquite and bitter sage but beyond that he saw nothing but flat, sunbaked ground. 'I don't see anything,' he said finally.

'It ain't likely you would. The trail we've been on goes straight ahead towards those hills on the horizon. If anyone does come after us, I'll wager that's the way they'll go. Sometimes the Indians hid their trails well, especially after the white man came. Both of you follow me.'

Wheeling his mount he headed straight for the mesquite. Not until they reached it did Mark spot the narrow gap through the tenacious plants. It was barely wide enough for a horse to pass through. On the far side were two large, flat rocks and beyond them the ground fell steeply away. Reining up his mount sharply, Calhoun pointed. Almost directly below them, the ground descended in a series of ledges with a narrow, twisting trail passing from one ledge to the next.

It looked both difficult and dangerous to negotiate but Calhoun unhesitatingly put his mount to it, edging slowly from one rim to the other. Gritting his teeth, Mark followed. He could sense the nervousness in his mount but somehow it retained its footing on the treacherous surface. Behind him, Della followed.

The minutes passed with a nightmare slowness as they descended the slope. At any moment, Mark expected his mount to slip, to go sliding down the almost sheer side but, somehow, they made it to the bottom. Here, the sheer wall extended for more than 200 yards in either direction. Along its length he noticed a number of darkly shadowed caves cut back into the rock.

He opened his mouth to ask what they were but before he could put the question, Calhoun said quietly, 'Some of the old Indians lived in these caves rather than out on the open plains. That was centuries ago. They've now been abandoned for ages.'

Dropping from the saddle, he led his mount to the nearest, motioning to Mark and Della to follow him. The cave extended back for almost thirty feet with plenty of room for them and the horses.

'Bring some of that dry sage, Mark,' Calhoun said. 'We'll soon have a fire going.'

'Is that wise?' Della asked. 'Smoke could be seen for miles.'

'Not from in here,' her grandfather told her, 'and we might as well have some hot grub before we set out again.'

'When are you thinkin' of riding on again?' Mark asked.

'Once it's dark,' the old man replied.

With that, Mark had to be content. Going outside, he gathered a large handful of the withered sage and brought it back. Inside the cavern the air was cold but Calhoun soon had a warm blaze going in the middle of the floor.

Once he had eaten his fill, Mark asked, 'How long before those bounty hunters discover you're no longer in Henders Rock and come lookin' for you, Frank?'

Chewing on a strip of bacon, the old man reflected on that for a moment, then said drily, 'Not long, I guess. But they won't find it easy. I've got a little place up in those hills yonder. If they trail me there, they're finished. One man could hold that place against an army.'

'And these men,' Mark persisted, 'what did you do to get your picture on these wanted posters?'

For a moment he thought the other did not intend to give him an answer. He was silent for so long that it was Della who said first, 'He shot down two men in self-defence in Oregon. There was a bank robbery and those four swore he was the leader.'

'So now you're on the run,' Mark said.

'That's right.' Calhoun gave a nod. Getting to his feet, he continued, 'Think you can make it back to the top, Mark? Before we ride for the hills, I need to know if we're bein' followed. The fact we've got so far without any sign worries me.'

'I'll make it.' Going out, Mark threw an appraising glance at the steep slope and then commenced to climb. At the top, he threw himself down onto the flat rocks, parting the thick mesquite. From his vantage point he could see the whole length of the trail, clear through the wide canyon.

It seemed empty but then, lifting his gaze slightly, squinting against the vicious sunlight, he made out a small group of men. They were still more than three miles away but riding fast. Ignoring the sharp edges of rock he slid back down.

'Riders coming,' he said sharply.

'How far?' Calhoun asked. He kicked dust onto the fire.

'Quite a ways. They ain't entered the canyon yet but there's no doubt they're headed this way.'

'Could you make out how many there are?' Della enquired. For a moment there was an expression of alarm on her face but it was gone within a moment.

Mark shook his head. 'It was hard to tell in the sunlight but I reckon there are at least half a dozen.'

Calhoun led the way to the waiting mounts. 'Then if they are those bounty hunters, they must have got others to come with 'em.'

'They could be Corby's men,' Mark suggested. 'I guess he wants me just as badly as those men want you.'

Grim-faced, Calhoun muttered, 'Whoever it is we have to reach those hills before they catch us, otherwise you'll have to use those guns whether you know how or not. Leastways they won't see our dust from there.'

Mounting up, they moved away from the tall rise. Ahead of them lay a parched wilderness where little grew. It blazed in the harsh sunglare. Here and there were clumps of Spanish thorn and the over-present tumbleweeds rolling across the flat landscape. None of them spoke as they pushed their mounts to the limit. All around them the air shimmered like water, distorting details.

Half an hour later they came upon a wide riverbed. Like the country around it, this was dried up with only a shallow trickle of water running over stones. On the far bank, they paused to glance behind them. What he saw sent a shiver of apprehension through Mark. Somehow those riders had picked up their trail and were now less than four miles away, still spurring their mounts to a cruel pace.

Ahead of them the hills still seemed as far way as ever. 'We'll never make it,' he muttered. 'And as far as I can see there's no cover around here.'

'Then we'll find some,' Calhoun said grimly. Wheeling his mount he kicked spurs to its flanks. Swiftly, Mark and Della followed. Scanning the terrain through red-rimmed eyes, Mark could see no place where they might make a stand against their pursuers. However, there was nothing they could do but follow Calhoun's lead. Inwardly, Mark wondered just how well the outlaw knew this region.

At the moment, the other had angled away from their original path and was heading in a more westerly direction. Not until a further five minutes had passed did he recognize that Calhoun was making for a line of small buttes. They ran together, showing as a hog's back rising some ten feet from the flatness of the plain. As they reached them, Calhoun slipped from the saddle on the run, pulling his Winchester from the scabbard. Slapping his mount on the flanks, the old man headed for the nearest mass of rock.

Dismounting swiftly, Mark and Della followed. Here there was a long rift in the ground some twelve feet long and five feet in width. Dropping down into it, Mark tugged the Colts from their holsters. They felt heavy and awkward in his hands.

Turning his head, Calhoun said sharply, 'Spread out and keep your heads down.'

Crouching down, Mark moved along the rocky channel. Cautiously, an inch at a time, he raised his head until his eye level was just above the lip of the rift. The riders were still approaching but now they were more cautious, not quite sure where they were.

A moment later, a rifle shot rang out. One of the leading riders suddenly threw up his arms and pitched from the saddle. 'Guess I ain't lost my knack with a Winchester,' Calhoun said grimly.

Two hundred yards away, the rest of the men had pulled their horses to a halt, sliding from the saddle and dropping onto the dirt. Several revolver shots rang out, the slugs kicking up dust in front of Mark. Resting his wrist on the rock, he levelled one of the Colts. One of the men suddenly lurched to his feet, the Colt in his hand spat twice. Mark sucked in a harsh gasp of air as a slug scorched along his cheek. Swiftly, without taking conscious aim, he squeezed the trigger and felt the recoil hammer along his arm.

He saw the man stagger as the slug took him in the left shoulder. Della too had a Winchester pressed into her shoulder. Two of the men attempted to rush them, weaving from side to side to present more difficult targets. Della fired twice, instinctively switching her aim. The two shots rang out so quickly that they blended into a single hammer of sound.

Both men came to a halt as if they had simultaneously run into an invisible wall. Their legs jerking from the knees, they went down.

The gunslinger Mark had hit was still on his feet, his features a mask of pain and fury. He came lurching forward, swaying drunkenly as he struggled to bring his gun to bear. Without thinking, Mark squeezed the trigger again but the slug went wide.

Then the gunhawk was only five paces away, his thick lips drawn back across his teeth as he levelled his Colt at Mark's head, his finger tight on the trigger. With a sudden cry, Mark flung himself back.

Through wide, staring eyes, he recognized the man as the one called Jed who had tried to call him out in the saloon. Desperately, he tried to lift the Colt, to squeeze the trigger but his finger wouldn't move. Utter fear held him paralysed. Then a shot rang out. He flinched at the sound and several moments fled before he realized he was still alive.

In front of him Jed suddenly buckled at the waist, staring stupidly at the spreading red stain on the front of his shirt. A long sigh came from his slack lips as he toppled forward over the ledge, his head less than an inch from Mark's, his unseeing eyes staring into his face.

Glancing round as he pulled himself away from the body, he noticed the smoking Winchester in

Della's hands. 'Thanks.' Somehow he got the word out.

It was then he grew aware that the gunfire had stopped. Pushing himself to his feet he stared into the glare of the sunlight. Only two of the gunhawks remained on their feet and both were struggling to get back into the saddle.

Aiming swiftly, Calhoun sent a couple of shots after them as they raced away. One of the men jerked abruptly but somehow remained in the saddle.

Getting to his feet, the old man clambered out of the rift and walked forward, both Colts ready in his hands as he examined the four bodies lying in the dust. Finally satisfied, he came back. Glancing at Mark, he grinned. 'For someone who's never handled a gun in his life you didn't do too badly, young fella,' he said firmly. 'I reckon we've seen the last o' these gunslicks for a while. Guess they got more'n they bargained for.'

Mark prodded the dead man beside him. 'This one was in the saloon last night,' he remarked. 'These must be some o' Corby's men.'

Calhoun scratched his cheek. 'Somehow, I reckon those bounty hunters won't be too pleased about this. They won't be wantin' to share any o' that reward money with Corby's hired gunmen.'

Mark forced a grin. 'I don't think Corby will like it either. So long as I'm alive he can't get his hands on the deeds to the land.'

Della's face assumed a serious expression. 'I wouldn't bank on that too much, Mark. Corby is well in with Simmins, the lawyer. My guess is it won't take them long to cook up something.'

'She's right, son,' Calhoun said. 'All Corby has to do is tell the county judge that you're a wanted outlaw and therefore no longer the legal owner o' that spread. If he does that and takes it over, you won't find it easy to get it back.'

Lips pressed into a tight line, Mark thought that over for a little while, then gritted, 'I reckon the sooner you show me how to use these guns, the better, Frank.'

CHAPTER IV

INTRIGUE

Sheriff McKinrick was seated behind his desk eating his lunch when the street door was thrust open and Seth Corby walked in. Behind him was a shorter, sallow-faced man dressed in a black tail-coat.

Without preamble, Corby said harshly, 'I guess you know Mr Simmins, Sheriff.'

McKinrick nodded. 'I know him,' he replied shortly. He stared directly at the rancher. 'You got some legal business here?'

Corby gave an oily smile. 'I like to see that everything is conducted strictly accordin' to the law.' His tone changed slightly. 'You put out that wanted notice for young Kennick yet?'

'It ain't been printed yet,' the lawman snapped. 'And so far, I ain't heard Kennick's side o' this shootin' in the saloon.'

'Nor are you likely to, Sheriff.' Without being invited, he sat down in the chair facing McKinrick.

'Since you didn't see fit to round up a posse and go after him when he rode out o' town, I sent some o' my boys to bring him back for trial.'

'Then where is he? I don't see him here.'

Clenching his fists, Corby leaned forward over the desk. 'I sent six men to bring that killer in and only two came back.'

Surprise showed momentarily on the lawman's lined features. 'You're sayin' that one man who's never handled a gun in his life took on six o' your hired gunslingers and killed four of 'em?'

'No, that ain't what happened. Kennick wasn't alone. There were three of 'em and one o' the others was Frank Calhoun. You've got his picture up there on the wall – a killer who's wanted in half-a-dozen states for murder and bank robbery.

'You don't need the evidence o' that killin' in the saloon, Sheriff. Anyone who teams up with a known outlaw becomes one too.'

The sheriff pushed his empty plate away. Rolling a cigarette, he ignored Simmins, and looked straight at Corby. 'Seems to me you're mighty anxious to get your hands on him. Couldn't be so that you can get hold of the deeds to that spread, I suppose?'

Standing a trifle nervously behind Corby, Simmins put in, 'As I see it that puts him outside o' the law. Wanted killers have no right to hold title to any land.'

McKinrick waved a match over the end of the cigarette and inhaled deeply. Through the smoke, he said, 'If that was true, Simmins, you'd find that most o' the ranchers in this territory have no rights to the land they've got.'

'Now see here, McKinrick, I—'

The sheriff held up his hand, silencing the other. 'All right, Corby. If Kennick has thrown in his lot with Calhoun, I'll go after 'em both. But if I do get him, I'll see that he gets a fair trial and ain't shot – supposedly tryin' to escape.'

Corby face flushed a deep red with suppressed anger but he said nothing. A moment later, he got to his feet and left with the lawyer trailing at his heels.

Across the street, four men were seated around a table in the Miners Hotel. All were dressed in similar attire, long frock coats and dark hats. Hal Dexter, tall and thin with a narrow face, sporting a pencil-thin moustache, removed the gold watch from his waistcoat pocket and studied it intently for a few moments before replacing it.

Looking up, he said tightly, 'Well gentlemen, I suggest we start makin' some enquiries around this helltown.'

To James Forbes, the stout man on his left, he went on, 'You check with the local sheriff, James. He should have received word about Calhoun by now from the authorities in Dawson.' Glancing across the table, he went on, 'I suggest that you, Sam, have a talk with the bartender in the saloon yonder.'

Sam Wellard gave a curt nod. His darkly handsome features assumed a sullen expression. Inwardly, he disagreed with the way in which Dexter had assumed command of the group as if the other had the right to give them orders. The one thing which kept him from speaking his mind was the lightning speed with which the other could draw his Colt and never miss his target.

Mel Dawson, the fourth man asked, 'What do you want me to do, Hal?'

'You can check with the hardware storekeeper. If Calhoun is somewhere in town, he'll need ammunition and it's likely he's been there at some time. I'll ride out and have a word with this Seth Corby. Seems he's the biggest man in this town and such men make it their business to know every gunman who rides in.'

Going out onto the boardwalk, Dexter unhitched his mount and climbed into the saddle. He sat there for a moment and watched as his three companions went their separate ways, then gigged the bay along the street following the directions he had been given the previous evening.

He spotted the ranch house half an hour later. It lay in a small valley, a large building built in the old colonial style. Evidently, he thought, Corby was a very wealthy man. Slowly, he followed the wide trail down the hillside. He was still 200 yards from the courtyard fronting the building when two men stepped out of the trees.

Both held rifles in their hands. The taller of the two said harshly, 'This is Corby land, mister. What's your business here?'

Drawing himself up in the saddle, keeping his hands in plain view, Dexter said, 'I'd like to have a few words with Mr Corby. My name's Cal Dexter.'

The second man stepped forward. His eyes held a look of suspicion. 'You some kind o' lawman, Dexter?

I don't see any star.'

'Nope. Let's just say that, with my partners, we bring in any wanted men, dead or alive.'

The first man's eyes narrowed at that remark. 'A goddamn bounty hunter. I should've known it. If you're lookin' to take in any men workin' for Mr Corby, you're on the wrong trail, mister.

Dexter forced a thin smile. 'I reckon the man I'm after won't be workin' here. I—'

'Just who is it you're after?' The voice came from just behind Dexter. Swinging in the saddle, he noticed the man who had ridden up so silently he hadn't picked out a sound.

'I'm Seth Corby,' the man said harshly. 'You got somethin' you want to say to me?'

Dexter nodded. He flashed a glance at the two gunmen nearby. 'If we could talk in private.'

Corby considered that and then gave a nod. 'All right. Come along to the house.'

Pushing his mount past Dexter's, Corby led the way into the courtyard. Taking the bounty hunter inside, he nodded towards one of the chairs at the long oak table.

Bringing a bottle and two glasses, he seated himself opposite Dexter, poured two drinks, then said, 'What is it you want to see me about, Mister—'

'Cal Dexter,' the other said smoothly. 'I suppose you would call me a bounty hunter, Mr Corby. I'm on the trail of an outlaw named Calhoun and I've reason to believe he's somewhere in Henders Rock. I was hopin' you might be able to help me locate him.'

Corby took out a cigar pouch, extracted one and

offered it to Dexter, taking another for himself. After lighting them, he said, 'If I tell you where Calhoun is, there's somethin' I want you to do for me in return.'

'What would that be?' Dexter asked. 'Perhaps I should say I have three partners with me already makin' discreet enquiries in town.'

Corby made a negligent gesture with his cigar. 'I ain't lookin' for any o' the reward money. But there's a man now ridin' with Calhoun, fellow by the name o' Kennick. I want him dead and I need proof o' that. Six o' my men went after him yesterday and only two came back. Kennick is no gunman so my guess is that Calhoun killed 'em.'

Dexter drew deeply on his cigar. 'That seems a fair proposition to me, Corby. All you want is for us to bring back Kennick, dead or alive.'

'Exactly,' Corby nodded. 'but preferably dead.'

'So where exactly are these men?'

'My men trailed 'em to the north o' here, came up with them in the middle o' the badlands there. My guess is they're headed for the hills some ten miles from here. It's possible Calhoun has some hidin' place there.'

Dexter pursed his lips, staring down at the glowing tip of his cigar. 'It shouldn't be too difficult flushin' them out with four of us. Once that's done, we get the reward and you get this man you want.'

'I reckon I can let you have two or three o' my men to ride along with you.'

Taking another draw of his cigar, Dexter shook his head. 'That won't be necessary. We've hunted down men faster with a gun than Calhoun. He's an old man now, well past his prime and you say this Kennick fellow is no gunman.'

'Far as I know, he's never handled a gun in his life.'

As he left the ranch to ride back into town, Dexter wondered a little about Kennick and why Corby was so desperate for him to be killed. Then he put the thought out of his mind. Another dead man made no difference to him and his colleagues. All that counted was bringing in Calhoun and collecting the reward.

Back in the hotel he found the other three waiting for him. As he sat down, Forbes said, 'I didn't get much out o' the sheriff, Cal. He admitted that Calhoun was in town but that was all.'

'And I guess you got the same information from the barkeep and that store owner,' Dexter said thinly.

As the other two nodded, he went on, 'Well, as it happens, I did get something from that rancher, Corby. Calhoun is hidin' out in the hills to the north. Some o' Corby's men ran into him in the badlands there and four of 'em got killed for their trouble.'

'And how far can you trust this rancher?' Wellard enquired. 'Men like that don't give out such information without wantin' something in return.'

Running a hand down his cheek, Dexter said, 'Seems Calhoun ain't on his own. There's a greenhorn ridin' with him by the name o' Kennick. Corby wants us to kill him and bring the body back here as proof that he's dead.'

Dawson twisted his lips into a puzzled frown. 'Why would he want that?'

Dexter shrugged. 'I didn't bother to ask. That's his business. Another dead man won't make any difference to us. We just do as I agreed. Now I suggest we get some supplies. We'll head for the hills in a couple o' days.'

Glancing up Wellard said gruffly, 'Why waste time? It'll only take an hour to get supplies and we can leave tonight.'

'Sure we can and leave ourselves open to an ambush. Those badlands are open ground for miles. You can be sure Calhoun will be watchin' every inch o' the way. He'll be ready for us. No, we wait until there's no moonlight. My guess is that Calhoun figures he's safe, holed up in those hills.'

Forbes gave a nervous cough. 'The question is, does he know we're in town? So far he's been hit only by this rancher's men.'

Dexter shook his head. 'I can't see how he can possibly know that. There's no one in this town likely to get word to him.'

Darkness was moving in from the east when Calhoun led the way into the dense stand of trees at the foot of the hills. With no pursuit, they had taken their time crossing the arid wasteland, leaving their mounts to pick their own pace. All of the horses were tired and Calhoun did not risk pushing them too hard.

Mark sat slumped forward over the stallion's neck. His throat was parched and the dust had congealed with the sweat on his body, itching intolerably. By now, he reckoned those two survivors from the force

Corby had sent after him would have reported back to the rancher. Without a doubt this news would make Corby even more determined to get him.

Lifting his head slowly, he surveyed the hills in front of them. As far as he could judge they stretched away for several miles in either direction. All of the lower slopes were covered with firs and dense vegetation. Only the topmost crests showed clearly in the light of the setting sun.

Calhoun had certainly chosen this place well, he thought dully. Unless he knew these hills thoroughly, a man could get lost in the dense forest which covered them. A man with the outlaw's intimate knowledge of the region could ambush anyone attempting to trail him.

Keeping their heads low to avoid overhanging branches, he and Della followed the old man deeper into the trees. If there was a track here only Calhoun could see it. Moving in the lead, the old man turned his mount several times apparently at random. Yet he seemed to know where he was going.

Now they were climbing steadily, moving towards the summits. Several times they were forced to halt as the weary animals slipped on the treacherous ground among the trees. Then, without warning, they emerged onto a wide rocky shelf. Here, Calhoun swung his mount to the left. Turning in the saddle, he called, 'Not far now. Then we'll be able to rest. There's a spring close by for fresh water.'

Wiping the sweat from his face, Mark hauled himself upright in the saddle. Inwardly, he wondered how Della managed to keep up with them. Glancing sideways he noticed the lines of strain and weariness on her features.

The cabin which showed through the trees was sturdily built of pine logs. It had a look of age about it and, as Calhoun had said, there was a narrow stream tumbling down the hillside within a few feet of it.

Dismounting, Calhoun said, 'I came upon this place more'n fifteen years ago. Guess it was some old hunter's shack in the old days before the war. Now nobody ever comes here and I reckon few folk know it exists.'

He pointed to his right. 'As you can see, it has a view over the whole of the badlands. Anyone comin' this way can be spotted long afore they reach the hills.'

'Unless they decide to come at night,' Mark said. 'Then it won't be so easy.'

'True,' Calhoun admitted. 'But only a fool would attempt to negotiate this trail through the hills in the dark. One slip and they'd go all the way to the bottom.'

'Let's hope you're right,' Della said as she slid from the saddle. 'Right now I guess we could all do with something to eat.' She went into the shack and Mark could hear her moving around, rattling pots and pans.

Turning to Mark, Calhoun said, 'Let me see those Colts o' yours.'

Taking them from their holsters, Mark handed them to him. In the half-light, Calhoun studied them for a moment, hefting them in his hands. Then he pulled open the chambers and let the remaining cartridges fall into one hand.

Motioning Mark to replace the empty guns, he stood a little way in front of him. 'There are two things you've got to learn if you're face to face with someone intent on killin' you,' he said thinly. 'To get them clear o' leather as fast as possible and to aim straight without squintin' along the barrel. You fire from the hip. You got that?'

Mark nodded. 'I reckon so.'

'Then first you're goin' to practise the draw. By the time I'm finished with you, I want those guns out and levelled before I can draw my own. It'll take time but I think you've got it in you. Just bear in mind I ain't aiming to make an outlaw of you. I'm doin' this because when you do come up against those killers, and you will unless you ride clear out o' the territory, it'll be either you or them lyin' dead in the street.'

The old man watched attentively as Mark went through the motions again and again. Endlessly, the hammers clicked on empty chambers. By the time Della called them inside, his wrists were aching but he was getting the hang of drawing the Colts smoothly from the holsters. They no longer felt a strange, unnatural part of him.

Over the course of the next two days Mark went through the same routine; drawing the Colts and lining them up on Calhoun's chest as the old man stood in front of him, his keen eyes watching and assessing every move.

Finally, he put his hand into his pocket and drew out the slugs, handing them over. 'Load them,' he said. 'Then we'll see how good your aim is.' Going into the shack, he brought out three empty cans and placed them on a low branch at the far end of the clearing.

Coming back, he said, 'Don't tense yourself. Loosen up your arms and shoulders. Fix your eyes on those cans, level the guns and squeeze the triggers all in the same movement.'

Pulling the Colts from leather, Mark lifted the barrels and squeezed off two shots. One of the cans fell. The other shot missed tearing a slice of bark from the branch.

'Again,' Calhoun ordered. This time both slugs went wide of their targets.

Clapping Mark on the shoulder, the old man said, 'Don't get disheartened, boy. You'll get the hang of it yet. All you need is practice. Believe me, it took me a long while but from what I see you're a born gunman to have achieved this in just a few days.'

He turned to where Della stood in the doorway. 'She took to a rifle like a duck to water.' Pausing, he studied Mark gravely, then went on, 'I understand your pa not wantin' guns in the house but when you head out into this territory you need to carry a weapon. This is still lawless country and a man has a right to defend himself. From what I hear, what happened at your place was cold-blooded murder.'

The bitterness came back to Mark's face. 'That's why I aim to kill those men who did it – and Corby too.'

Nodding in acquiescence, Calhoun gave a tight-lipped smile. 'That's why I'm doin' this. I don't like to see a man not given a fair chance.'

Seth Corby was seated at his usual table in the saloon staring down at the cards in his hand. The previous day he had sent Simmins on the stage to Twin Springs thirty miles away with orders to speak with the circuit judge. The fact that Mark Kennick had joined up with this notorious outlaw meant that he had to change his original plans.

Somehow, he doubted if those bounty hunters would have any more success in hunting down the two men than his own men had. Word had been brought to him that the four men were still at the hotel. Clearly they weren't in a hurry to go after Calhoun and Kennick.

Furthermore, Calhoun had evaded the law in several states for a number of years. Now he was forced to accept the remote possibility that this young whippersnapper might return to Henders Rock and persuade a jury that he had acted in self-defence. If that should happen, his chances of getting that land were virtually zero.

However, once the lawyer persuaded the judge to allow him to take over the spread after declaring Kennick a wanted killer, he would feel easier in his mind. Then he could move in, rebuild the burnt-out house and put some of his cattle on the land. In this wild country possession was more than nine tenths of the law.

Even in the eventuality that Kennick was declared innocent, he would find few of the townsfolk willing to back him against a dozen hired gunmen. He still had Dominguez and the other three gunmen he could count on.

'Are you in this game, Seth?' Devaroux's question jerked his thoughts back to the present.

Nodding, Corby raised the stakes and sat back, trying to concentrate. The stage from Twin Springs was due to arrive in town within an hour. With any luck, Simmins would be on it with good news.

The poker game was almost over when the lawyer stepped through the doors of the saloon. His thin features were inscrutable as he crossed over to the table and stood just behind Corby's chair. The rancher deliberately ignored him until he showed his last hand and scooped up his winnings.

Leaning forward slightly, he said, 'Deal me out o' this hand, gentlemen. I need to have a word with my lawyer.'

Taking Simmins by the arm, Corby led him to the bar, ordered two drinks, then said harshly, 'Well, did the judge do as you asked?'

Simmms swallowed nervously, his Adam's apple bobbing up and down in his scrawny throat. 'Not exactly, Mr Corby. He—'

'What do you mean, Simmins? You're supposed to know the law. If Kennick is a wanted killer, he has no right to that land.'

Simmins fiddled nervously with his glass and then gulped down half of the spirit. 'He said that so far he's seen no proof that Kennick did anything against the law. He said he personally knew the family and their aversion to weapons of any kind. If Kennick did use a gun, then it had to be in self-defence.'

Corby slammed his glass down on the bar, spilling half of the contents. 'I've got twenty men who'll swear that Kennick shot Ben in the back without givin' him a chance to draw. Did you tell him that? What more proof does that old fool want?'

Corby glared angrily at the rest of the whiskey in the glass and then downed it all in a single swallow.

'Did he say anything else?' he demanded.

'He said he intends to take the stage to Henders Rock two weeks from now to look into the whole affair, and that includes finding out how the Kennick family died.'

'So that's what he means to do.' A crafty look smouldered at the back of Corby's eyes. 'Then I'll have to make sure that the judge never reaches here. It's quite a way from Twin Springs to Henders Rock and a lot can happen on the trail. If that stage is held up somewhere along the route and we can get word around that this outlaw Calhoun and Kennick were responsible, that would solve everythin'.'

'You're not thinking o' killing the circuit judge, are you?' An expression of alarm flashed over the lawyer's angular face. 'If you do that, it'd bring a whole posse o' federal marshals down on our necks.'

'Can you think of a better plan?'

Simmins averted his gaze. 'I'm just pointing out the danger of such a move. Federal marshals poke into everythin' and if they should discover you brought in those gunhawks from across the border there'll be hell to pay.'

'They won't find anything,' Corby asserted confidently. 'I'll make sure of that.'

'Then I only hope you know what you're doin', because I want no part of it.' Turning on his heel, Simmins went out leaving Corby standing at the bar.

Corby remained at the bar for a few moments, deliberating his next move. Ignoring the three men at the card table, he went out onto the boardwalk, paused for a moment, and then walked across the street to the hotel.

He found the four bounty hunters seated around a table in the lounge. The fury at Simmins' failure to persude the judge to turn over the deeds of the Kennick place to him still rankled and some of the anger showed through in his voice as he said harshly, 'What are you four doin' still sittin' here? I thought we had an agreement. You'd bring in Kennick over a saddle and I'd see you get the reward for Calhoun.'

Dexter turned slightly. 'That isn't the way we work, Mr Corby. The way we do things is not to go charging in with all guns blazin'. That's what your men did, and see where it got 'em.'

Corby pressed his lips together into a hard line. 'Frankly, I don't give a damn how you work. I want Kennick dead and across a saddle in Henders Rock by tomorrow noon. You got that?'

At the other side of the table, Wellard shifted a little in his seat, deliberately drawing aside his frock coat to reveal the Colt at his waist. With a faint twist of his lips, he said smoothly. 'You heard what my friend said, Corby. There's a moon tonight and possibly a clear sky. We know Calhoun of old. He's a dangerous man which is why he's stayed alive for so long. He'll be watching the badlands like a hawk and we don't intend to ride into a trap.'

Swallowing hard, Corby tried to hide his anger. This was his town and he did not intend to have his wishes thwarted in this way. 'Then I reckon you'd better change your plans, gentlemen. I don't intend to wait much longer. Either you ride out tonight and get those two killers or—'

'Or what, Mr Corby?' Forbes put in.

'Or I get together twenty o' my men and we flush 'em out. That way you'll see not a dollar o' that reward money for Calhoun.'

Corby allowed his gaze to move from one man to the other. The expressions on their faces told him all he wanted to know. Greed would overcome any nervousness they might have of being ambushed.

Finally, Dexter gave an almost imperceptible nod. 'Very well. If you put it that way, we'll ride out as soon as it's dark.'

'Good. Somehow I figured you would. You only have Calhoun to worry about. The Kennick kid couldn't hit a man from ten feet. I'd say the odds are four to one in your favour.'

Feeling slightly more satisfied, Corby left. It would soon be dark and if these four men were true to their word, by tomorrow he would have little to worry about. With Kennick dead and declared a wanted outlaw, there would be no need for him to have the circuit judge ambushed and killed. Lighting a cigar, he puffed on it for a moment then walked back to the saloon.

*

Mark sat on a low rocky ledge and slowly built himself a smoke. Practising day in and day out until his wrists and arms ached, he was now almost as fast and accurate with a Colt as Calhoun. Lighting the cigarette, he blew a cloud of smoke into the air.

The anger and bitterness at what had happened to his family was still there, deep inside him but now it was overlaid by an icy calm. He knew exactly what he had to do and was fully determined to go through with it. Musingly, he thought it was strange how events could change a man's life completely in so short a time. Only a little while earlier he had been working on the farm with hardly a care in the world.

Now he was a wanted criminal, an outlaw, with both the law and Corby's men on his tail. No doubt, like Calhoun, his picture would be on the wall of the sheriff's office.

He turned sharply at a sudden soft sound behind him. Della came out of the shack and walked over to stand beside him. Even in the dimness he could see every line of her face clearly.

In a soft voice, she asked, 'You're still thinking about those men who murdered your family, Mark?'

He gave a slight nod. 'All I want now is to get each of those men in front of me with a gun and shoot them down like they did my sister. But this time, I won't shoot them in the back as they did with her. I want them to see who kills them and take my face with them into Hell.'

'Just be careful, Mark. Those men would just as readily shoot you from some dark alley in town as face you.'

Mark sat staring at the glowing tip of his cigarette, saying nothing. He knew that what Della said was true. Men such as these only faced down a man when they were certain the odds were stacked in their favour.

Looking up, he adroitly changed the subject. 'Why did you come out here with us, Della? Surely it would be far safer for you stayin' in town.'

He noticed a strange expression on her face as she replied, 'Both my father and mother were killed by gunmen when I was only eight. We were on the stage from Tucson when they attacked it. My mother fell on top of me and I guess those killers thought I was dead. It was left to my grandfather to bring me up.'

'And after what had happened, he taught you how to use that Winchester?'

'Yes. I know he's killed several men but always in fair fight. However, the law branded him an outlaw so we kept moving from one place to another, always just one step ahead of the law. I think he knew he'd be shot or hanged sometime and he was determined I knew how to protect myself.'

'If it's any consolation to you, I think he did right.'

Della stood looking down at him for a few moments and then went back into the shack.

Darkness fell quickly now that the sun had set. Towards the west the faint colours of the sunset were fading as the first sky sentinels came out overhead. There was a half moon just visible low in the east, throwing a pale light over the arid waste in the distance.

For some odd reason he could feel the tension

rising in him. Down below, the great stretch of the forest was quiet, too quiet. By the time he had smoked his third cigarette, it was beginning to get cold as the night chill swept up the hillside.

Getting up, he threw a last glance towards the badlands then stiffened abruptly. At first he thought he was mistaken, that his sight was playing tricks with him. Then, narrowing his eyes, he made out a small knot of figures just visible against the dark backdrop.

Swiftly, he called, 'Riders comin', Frank.'

Calhoun was standing in the doorway within seconds. 'How many?'

'Three, perhaps four. Difficult to be sure. They're still some distance away but definitely headin' in this direction.'

Moving swiftly, Calhoun ran over. Della was only a couple of feet behind him. Turning to his grand-daughter, Calhoun said sharply, 'Can you make them out, Della? Your eyesight is better'n mine.'

'I can see them. There are four and I'd say they're all wearing dark clothing.'

'Then it's those bounty hunters,' Calhoun snapped. 'I was wonderin' how long it would be before they came.'

'What do you aim to do, Frank?' Mark asked. 'Pull out or stay here and fight? They must be fools if they think they can reach us without bein' seen.'

Calhoun shook his head. 'They're no fools, Mark. I figured they'd wait until there was no moon but I guess someone has pressured 'em into takin' the risk.'

'You think it was Corby?'

Frank nodded. 'It couldn't have been anyone else. It was certainly not the sheriff. The law doesn't interfere with men such as these. It saves them the trouble of goin' after wanted men.'

Della said, 'There's still plenty of time for us to pull out and be miles away to the west by the time they get here.'

Calhoun turned. 'And you reckon they'd give up if they found us gone, Della? Once men like that get the scent, they stay with it to the end. We've got a far better chance o' defending ourselves here than out in the open. There's only an empty plain on the other side o' these hills.'

To Mark he said briskly, 'Get those horses among the trees out o' sight. Della, you get your rifle and plenty o' shells. The only way they can get here is through the trees and along this ledge. We can cover every approach from inside the shack and those walls will stop any bullet.'

Five minutes later they were crouched behind the two windows with a heavy steel bolt across the door. Outside, the silence was absolute. The minutes passed slowly and each one brought a heightening of the tension. Like a coiled spring inside him, it tightened the muscles of Mark's arms and shoulders as he crouched down in the darkness.

Calhoun must have noticed, for he said quietly, 'Relax, Mark. Don't forget what I've told you over the last few days. These men are really after me but you can bet Corby has talked them into killin' you.'

'Don't worry about me, Frank' Mark replied. 'You saved my life and I ain't going to forget that. I know what to do when they come.'

It was almost an hour later when Mark picked out a faint sound. It was the snicker of a horse somewhere among the trees facing the shack. Reaching out, he touched Calhoun's arm and saw the other nod.

A few moments later, a voice called, 'We know you're in there, Calhoun. Come out with your hands raised and you'll get a fair trial.'

'That goes for that other fellow you have with you,' shouted a second voice.

Keeping his voice to a whisper, Calhoun murmured, 'Don't say a word. This is an old trick o' theirs. They ain't fully sure that we're here with no sign o' the mounts. They just want us to give away our positions.'

The silence lengthened. Then, without warning a fusillade of shots rang out from among the trees. Slugs hammered against the wall of the shack and Mark pulled his head down sharply as the window shattered above his head, covering him with glass.

Outside, the moonlight was now sufficiently bright for the defenders to see the line of trees clearly. Risking a quick look, Mark spotted the lances of gunflame. The four men had spread themselves out among the trees and were keeping their heads down.

Beside him, Calhoun raised his head slowly. Aiming swiftly, he sent several shots into the trees. Mark distinctly heard a harsh gasp and knew that one of the slugs had found its target. Whether the man was dead or just wounded it was impossible to tell.

At the other window, Della was firing rapidly whenever she saw a movement. For the most part the bounty hunters were firing blindly, not daring to show themselves. Then there came a sudden lull in the gunfire.

Easing himself to one side of the window, Mark squinted into the moonlight. At first, he could see nothing. Among the trees there were only anonymous shadows. Carefully, he sighted the Colt on the spot where he had earlier spotted the bright spurts of muzzle flame.

Keeping his finger tight on the trigger, he waited. Then the concealed man showed his head as he shifted his position. Gently, Mark squeezed the trigger, firing three shots in quick succession. Scarcely had the racketing echoes died away than the head fell back out of sight and there was a crash in the undergrowth a moment later.

As he pulled his head back, Calhoun said, 'You got that one for sure, Mark.'

Sucking in a deep breath, Mark thrust fresh shells into the chamber of the Colt. 'There are still three of 'em out there,' he said shortly. 'You reckon they may try to rush us?'

'That ain't likely,' Calhoun replied grimly. 'We'd cut 'em down before they could reach the shack. They'll stay under cover and keep us pinned down. There's one thing we won't run short of – ammunition. I made sure I have plenty here just in case somethin' like this should happen.'

'You'd think they'd realize this will be a stand-off.'

Calhoun regarded him with a grim smile. 'Don't fool yourself, Mark. They've got the better position by far. We can only stay here at the windows. They can move anywhere in those trees and fire at us from almost any direction.'

With a conscious effort of will, Calhoun pushed himself to his feet, moving slightly to one side to get a better view of what was happening outside. His feet crunched loudly on the broken glass covering the floor. Balancing the Colts in his hands, he let his gaze rove over the long shadows, searching for the slightest movement that would give away the position of the men among the trees.

A second later, further shots erupted. Jerking up the Colts, Calhoun squeezed several shots, then staggered back, slumping against the wall. Quickly, Mark went down on one knee beside him. At the same time, he yelled, 'Keep watch at that window, Della. He's been hit in the right shoulder.'

For a moment, he thought the girl would disobey him. Then, a worried frown on her face, she turned back, keeping her head down.

'You were a goddamn fool exposin' yourself to their fire like that, Frank.' Mark spoke through his teeth as he pulled the other's jacket aside. Ripping open Calhoun's shirt, he examined the wound.

In the darkness it was difficult to see clearly but one glance told him that the slug was still in there. Staring around the cabin he noticed the white cloth lying on the table. Ducking his head, he reached it and tore off a long strip and used it to staunch the bleeding.

'I reckon you ain't going to do much shootin' with that arm for a while,' he said tautly. 'Just lie there or you'll bleed to death. Della and I will—'

He saw the look of alarm which flashed over the old man's grizzled face as the other stared over his shoulder. Swiftly, he rolled over onto his back, jerking the Colts from their holsters. The slug from Dexter's gun ricocheted off the floor between Mark and Calhoun.

In almost the same second, Mark squeezed both triggers. Both slugs took Dexter in the chest. For a moment, the bounty hunter remained upright, his face twisted into a look of amazement. Then his Colt fell from his fingers into the room as he slumped forward over the window.

Easing himself forward, Mark caught the dead man beneath the chest and heaved him out of the window. As he did so he made out the unmistakable sound of a horse crashing through the dense undergrowth, heading down the slope.

Silence returned as the echoes of the rider's flight faded into the distance. Mark let his breath go in a long exhalation. 'One of them got away,' he muttered, 'but I reckon we accounted for the other three. I'll go outside and check just to be certain.'

'Be careful, Mark.' Calhoun forced the warning out through tightly clenched teeth. 'This could be another trick to make us believe they're finished and get us out into the open. There could still be one o' the others left alive.'

'See what you can do for your grandfather, Della,' Mark said thinly. The icy calm he had felt earlier in the evening had now taken control of him again.

Opening the door, he moved out into the night.

The man he had shot at the window now lay on the rocks, his arms and legs outspread as if he had been crucified. One glance was enough to tell Mark he was dead.

Keeping his head down, he turned and ran for the trees, throwing himself down into the undergrowth. A little part of his mind told him that if either of those two remaining bounty hunters was still alive, he could expect a bullet at any moment. But none came. Slowly, he crawled forward, working his way among the trees.

A couple of minutes later, he came upon a body lying next to the trunk of a tall fir. A bullet had taken him between the eyes and Mark guessed this was the one he had shot. Several yards further on he found another. Turning him over, he saw the blood on the white shirt and a thin trickle which had oozed from the corner of the man's mouth.

Getting to his feet he went back to the shack. Della was kneeling beside her grandfather. She looked up as he entered.

'All but one of them is dead,' he said, in answer to her look of mute enquiry. Going over to the table, he lit the lamp. 'How is he?'

'The bullet is still in his shoulder but it will have to come out. He needs a doctor.' She got up. 'I'll have to ride into town and bring Dr Hamilton. He's a good friend of mine. I know he'll come and ask no questions.'

Mark shook his head. 'It's too dangerous, Della. For all we know that fourth bounty hunter is somewhere along the trail back into Henders Rock. If you should run into him, or any of Corby's men they'll—'

'None of these men know Frank is my grandfather. All they know is that I sing in the saloon.'

'And won't they think it's strange you haven't been there for the last few days?'

Delia's eyes flashed as she faced him. 'Can you take that bullet out and be sure he lives?' she demanded hotly. 'No, I don't think so. Neither can I. Now don't try to stop me. I know my way around Henders Rock and I can reach the doctor without anyone seeing me. As for that killer who escaped – he'll be miles away by now. Somehow I doubt if the thought of all that reward money will keep him in town.'

'I only hope you're right.' Mark knew there was no point in arguing any further with her. 'All right. Help me get your grandfather into a chair. Then do what you have to. I'll keep watch here in case that *hombre* does decide to come back.'

Five minutes later, Mark stood at the door of the shack and watched as Della put her mount into the trees.

CHAPTER V

NEWBORN GUNMAN

Cursing to himself as he rode across the arid flats, Sam Wellard kicked spurs cruelly into his mount's flanks, forcing the animal to the limit of its endurance. Everything that had happened had been Corby's fault, insisting they should set out in moonlight. He did not doubt they had been spotted long before they had reached the hills.

Calhoun had holed himself up with that other gunman in a virtually impregnable position and had been ready for them. Had they been allowed to do this job their own way, none of this would have happened.

Something moved just a short distance away and he jerked himself upright in the saddle, pulling the Colt from its holster. Slitting his eyes, he saw that it was nothing more than a large tumbleweed rolling across the flat ground. He swore again under his breath.

He was getting jumpy now and that was something he did not like. Thrusting the weapon back, he tried to think clearly and coherently but his thoughts were in a turmoil.

With his three companions now dead, he realized there were only two options open to him. Either he stayed on in Henders Rock in the hope that Calhoun might ride into town and he might still claim that reward – or he skirted the town and kept on riding.

The thought of all that reward money slipping through his fingers galled him. Now that Dexter and the other two were gone, all of it would be his. By the time the lights of Henders Rock came into sight, he had made up his mind. He would stay.

Pacing up and down in the cabin, the waiting seemed interminable. Calhoun sat slumped in the chair, his head drooping forward onto his chest. He was asleep and Mark guessed this was for the best. He had lost quite a lot of blood and occasionally a low moan would escape from his lips as the pain penetrated deep into his sleeping mind.

Going to the door, he listened intently for the sound of approaching horses which would tell him Della was returning with the doctor. But no sound broke the deep, eternal stillness of the hills. It was now almost two hours since she had left. Surely, he thought, if she hadn't run into any kind of trouble she should have been back by now.

He didn't doubt her ability to slip unnoticed into town and reach the doctor's surgery. But there was that fourth bounty hunter to be taken into account. It was possible the man had ridden hell for leather back to Henders Rock, perhaps afraid that they might come after him. On the other hand, he might still be lurking somewhere along the trail and if Della ran into him, she could be in big trouble.

A sudden sound from Calhoun brought him back into the room. The old man was attempting to rise to his feet. Gently, Mark pushed him back. Calhoun's face was grey beneath the weather-beaten tan.

For a moment, his lips moved but no sound came out. Then he muttered feebly. 'Has Della got back with the doctor?'

'Not yet.' Mark tried to inject reassurance into his voice. 'She won't be long. Just you lie still or that wound will start bleedin' again.'

'How long has she been gone?'

'A couple of hours. Could be she's havin' trouble persuadin' the doc to come back with her.'

With an effort, Calhoun heaved himself up in the chair. 'You got a smoke, Mark?'

Rolling one, Mark thrust it between the other's lips and lit it for him. Drawing on it, the old man said, 'You'll find some whiskey in the cupboard yonder. We might as well have a drink while we're waitin'.'

Mark could see that the old man was in a bad way. His lips were drawn back across his teeth as further spasms of pain lanced through him. Getting the whiskey, he poured some into a glass and handed it to the other.

Pouring one for himself, he had just put it to his lips when there came a sudden call from somewhere outside. Hefting the Colt in his right hand, he moved to the door, taking care not to show himself. Then he noticed the two riders at the far end of the rocky ledge, saw the moonlight glint on dark hair.

Reining up, Della dismounted swiftly and then turned to help the other rider down, taking the bag that the doctor handed to her. Hamilton was a short, grey-haired man in his mid-sixties. He gave a momentary start as he saw the body lying just outside the window but made no comment. Entering the cabin, he threw Mark a curious glance as he brushed past him.

Bending, he examined Calhoun, then turned to glance at the smashed windows. 'Seems to me there's been a regular gunfight here, Della,' he said drily. 'And I'm surprised to find you here, Mark.'

'With Seth Colby out to kill me so that he can get his hands on the deeds to the spread, I have to choose my friends carefully, people I know I can trust.'

'Can you do anythin' for him Doctor?' Della asked.

'First thing I'll have to do is get that slug out of his shoulder.' Going over to his bag on the table, he pulled it open.

Weakly, Calhoun said, 'You know who I am, don't you, Doc?'

'Sure I know who you are. Frank Calhoun, the outlaw. I've seen your picture often enough in Sheriff McKinrick's office.'

'So what do you intend to do about it?' Della asked sharply.

Hamilton met her stare directly. 'I'm a doctor, Della. My job is to help people. It makes no difference to me who they are. I leave that to the law. Far as I'm concerned, he's just another man with a bullet in his shoulder. Now I suggest you get some water and boil it for me.'

He shifted his gaze to Mark. 'You can give him some more o' that whiskey. It'll help deaden the pain a little.'

Once Della had brought the water, he cleaned the blood away from the wound. Mark handed the whiskey bottle to Calhoun who took several swallows and then said hoarsely, 'Get on with it, Doc.'

Turning to Mark and Della, Hamilton said, 'You two hold his arms down. This ain't goin' to be easy.'

Calhoun clenched his teeth as the doctor began probing. Sweat stood out on his face but he made no sound. Several minutes passed before Hamilton uttered a satisfied exclamation. 'It's out,' he said. 'Now all I have to do is bandage it up. After that, you'll need rest. You got any food here? He'll be up and about in a couple o' days but it'll be some time before he can use that arm again.'

'We've got plenty o' food and water here, Doctor,' Della said.

Closing his bag with a snap, Hamilton said, 'You care to tell me what happened? I know you're no outlaw, Mark, but I can understand you wantin' revenge on those who murdered your family. Yet I find you here in cahoots with a wanted killer.'

'Can you think of anyone better to teach me how to use these guns? Calhoun saved my life when one o' Corby's men threatened to call me in the saloon.'

'And you, Della – where do you fit in?'

Della hesitated, then straightened. Defiantly, she said, 'Frank Calhoun is my grandfather. Four bounty hunters rode into town a few days ago determined to kill him. I rode out to warn him.'

'And where are these four men now?' Hamilton asked.

'Three of 'em are dead out there,' Mark told him. 'The fourth got away.'

'I figured somethin' like this must've happened. I spotted this man Wellard ridin' into town just before you came, Della.'

'Do you intend to report this to the sheriff?' Della looked straight at the doctor as she spoke. There was a pleading expression on her face.

Without hesitation, Hamilton shook his head. 'I take men as I find 'em. I've heard plenty o' stories about you, Calhoun. How many are true, I don't know. But to my way o' thinking, Seth Corby is as much of a killer as they say you are and I don't see the sheriff makin' any move against him.'

'Thanks, Doc,' Calhoun said faintly. 'I'll remember that.'

'As for you, Mark, my advice is to get as far from here as possible. Don't underestimate Seth Corby. He's a mighty big man. A lot o' men have tried to go against him. Those that ain't dead upped stakes and moved out. You can't fight all o' the men he's got on his payroll.'

'I'll bear that in mind, Doc.'

Hamilton shrugged. 'It would be better for you if you acted on it. That way you might stay alive.' Throwing an oblique glance in Della's direction, he went on, 'Try to talk some sense into him.'

'Somehow, I don't think anything I can say will make him change his mind.'

'Then I'll say no more. Make sure your grandfather keeps calm and gets plenty to eat. I've done all I can for him. Guess I'd better ride back into town before someone misses me and starts askin' awkward questions.'

Jamming his hat on to his head, he paused at the door. 'Far as anyone in Henders Rock is concerned, I ain't been here and I ain't seen any of you.'

'Thanks again,' Della said. 'If you like, I'll ride back into town with you.'

'No need to do that. Bein' the town doctor means that no one takes much notice of me unless they need patchin' up. It ain't uncommon for me to visit patients durin' the night.'

When Sam Wellard finally reached Henders Rock and reined up in front of the hotel, he found Corby standing on the boardwalk. Slowly, feeling the aches and bruises in his limbs from the long ride, he slid from the saddle.

As he looped the reins over the rail, the rancher stepped down into the street. 'I see you've come back alone, Wellard.' There was a trace of underlying menace in Corby's voice which the bounty hunter noticed at once. 'What happened out there?'

Wellard felt a sudden surge of anger pass through him at the other's tone. 'I figure you know that well enough.' He spat the words at the other man. 'We told you we'd do this job in our own time and way but you wouldn't have that. Calhoun must've spotted us while we were miles away. They were waitin' for us once we found their hidin' place.'

'So your three companions are dead and those two are still alive.'

'Damn you, Corby. This is all your fault. If you think you know so much, why all the questions?'

Stepping forward, Corby grasped the lapel of the other's frock coat, thrusting his face close up to Wellard's. Through his teeth, he hissed, 'Because when four men ride into my town and claim they can do somethin' for me and then fail miserably, I don't like it.'

Pulling himself free of the other's grasp, Wellard moved his hand quickly, grasping the Colt beneath his coat. Before he could draw it, Corby said harshly, 'Try to use that gun and you'll be dead before you can draw it. Take a look at the opposite boardwalk.'

Wellard turned his head slowly, still keeping his grip on the handle of the Colt. There were three men standing on the other boardwalk. All three of them had Winchesters to their shoulders, the weapons lined on him. Swallowing thickly, he forced himself to relax, releasing his grip on the Colt.

'Now you're showin' some sense,' Corby said, grinning viciously. 'Believe me, if you weren't still useful to me, you'd be dead by now.'

'If you think I'm going back into those hills to get

those men, you'd better think again.' Somehow, Wellard got the courage to get the words out. He knew this man would not hesitate to kill him if he didn't do what he said.

A couple of people passed them on the boardwalk and Corby waited until they were out of earshot before saying, 'Nothin' like that. I've decided to take care of them myself. Two weeks from now the circuit judge is goin' to be on the stage leaving Twin Springs. You're goin' to be on it and just to make certain you don't double-cross me and ride out, one of my boys will accompany you.'

Wellard's face assumed a perplexed expression. 'I don't get it. You want me to ride out to Twin Springs and then take the stage back?'

'That's exactly what you'll do. Somewhere along the trail you'll stop the stage and take the judge off. It's goin' to took like a hold-up. Your job will be to make sure that Judge Torbin doesn't make it to Henders Rock.'

'I'm to kill the circuit judge?' Wellard shook his head. 'I'll never make it.'

'There'll be a mount waitin' for you and once he's dead my man will give you five thousand dollars. You're a sensible man, Wellard. You know you'll never get that reward money for Calhoun. With this you can be over the Mexican border with enough to live on for the rest o' your life.'

Wellard took out his handkerchief and mopped his face. He was sweating profusely. 'And if somethin' should go wrong?' he muttered.

'Nothin' will go wrong if you keep your part o' the

94

bargain. Besides, one o' my men will be with you. He'll swear you never pulled a gun.'

Corby moved away into the darkness. Over his shoulder he called, 'And don't try to leave town. I'll have someone watchin' you day and night. If you should try that, you'll be dead before you reach either end o' the street.'

Reaching out, Wellard grasped the nearby wooden upright. He knew that the rancher meant every word he had said. What had promised to be a simple job when he and his companions had ridden into Henders Rock had now turned into a nightmare and he could see no way out of it. Going into the hotel, he curtly ordered the barman to bring him a bottle of whiskey and a glass.

Approaching the town from the north, Della Calhoun edged her mount slowly along the narrow alley which ran parallel with the main street. Both Mark and her grandfather had been against her riding back into town. However, she had pointed out that only good fortune had prevented them from being surprised by the bounty hunters and it was essential they should have some information as to what was going on if they were not to be attacked again.

Since Mark would be instantly recognized, it had seemed only logical she should be the one to go. On the way to town, she had turned over in her mind the names of those she could trust. She knew the doctor would not betray them to anyone. In addition, Ed Clayton had helped Mark and been a good friend of his father's. Finally, she decided on checking with him. Reaching the end of the alley, she led her mount to the rear of the hardware store. Trying the back door, she found it was unlocked and after a quick glance all around, she slipped inside.

The door at the far end of the small room was partially open and as she approached it, she made out voices from the store beyond. Pressing herself against the wall, she opened the door a little further and peered through.

Sheriff McKinrick was there with Ed Clayton. The lawman was saying, 'You're sure you ain't seen the Kennick boy since you sold him those guns?'

'I've never set eyes on him since that mornin', Sheriff. Far as I know he intended ridin' out o' town that day.'

'Well he certainly didn't do that,' McKinrick said harshly. 'Seems he was in the saloon that night and when he did ride out it was with Frank Calhoun.'

'The outlaw?'

'That's right. I've got a feelin' he might try to sneak back into town. If he does, you let me know.'

'Sure thing, Sheriff.'

McKinrick paused for a moment, then turned and went out. Della waited for a moment and then went in. Clayton whirled quickly, then relaxed. 'What in tarnation are you doin' here, Della?'

'I need to talk to you, Ed. It's important.'

Clayton hesitated for a moment, then walked to the door, locking it and reversing the sign to indicate the shop was closed. 'In the back room, Della. We can talk there.'

Closing the door behind him, he motioned her to a chair at the small table. 'Is it somethin' about Mark Kennick?' he asked. 'When I last saw him he was all fired up, determined to go after those men who killed his family. I warned him against it but he crossed to the saloon that night. That was the last time I saw him.'

'He's quite safe for the moment, Ed.'

Clayton rubbed a hand across his forehead. 'Is it true what they say in town – that he's in cahoots with that outlaw, Frank Calhoun?'

'There's something I have to tell you, Ed, and I hope you'll take my word for what I'm about to say and keep it to yourself.'

'You can rely on me, Della, and if there's any way I can help Mark, I'll do it.'

Moistening her lips, she said, 'Frank Calhoun is my grandfather. I know he's shot several men in the past but it was always in fair fight and self-defence. Those stories that he's a bank robber are all lies. If they were true, he wouldn't be living in this territory now. He'd be across the border in Mexico.

'Those men who rode in a few days ago were bounty hunters, looking for the reward. When Seth Corby heard of this, he saw his chance to kill Mark. He told those men where they're hiding up in the hills. They attacked us last night. We killed three of them. The fourth is somewhere in town.'

'So what do you want me to do?'

'Corby is planning something, some way of getting those deeds Mark has, and we have to know what it is. You know most of what's happening in town, Ed. You can find out things that no one else can because no one suspects you.'

Clayton held her glance with an effort. After a moment, he said, 'There's one thing Mark might like to know. Corby's moved some of his cattle onto the Kennick spread and there's talk he's bringin' in men and materials to rebuild that burnt-out house.'

'You're sure of that?'

'Dead sure. A couple of his men were in the store yesterday pickin' up some shells. They weren't hidin' anything so my guess is that Corby's now mighty sure of himself. Another thing I heard from the sheriff: the circuit judge is due in town just over a week from now.'

'Do you have any idea why he's coming?' A worried frown momentarily creased Della's forehead. 'It isn't as if there's anyone in jail awaiting trial.'

'I know. But in the old days, Judge Torbin was a federal marshal and a good friend o' the Kennick family. Could be that Corby has tried to get him to declare Mark an outlaw, but he's decided to come here and see things for himself. If he does, he might start askin' awkward questions as to how the Kennick family died.'

Della bit her lower lip. If what Clayton was saying was true, it would mean that all hell could break loose in town and Corby could find himself in the middle of it. The rancher couldn't allow the circuit judge to start probing too deeply into what was going on otherwise the state law might move in.

'I think I'd better get this news back to my grandfather and Mark,' she said abruptly.

As she opened the rear door, Clayton said sharply, 'I don't know whether I should tell you this in case Mark tries to take the law into his own hands and gets himself shot.'

'What is it?'

'Last time I saw him, he asked if I'd seen four strangers around town, one of 'em a Mexican by the name of Pedro. Fact is, I've seen men answerin' that description several times in the saloon over the past few days. Word is that Corby brought 'em in from across the border.'

Nodding, Della said, 'I'll tell him. I guess it's up to him what he does about it.'

As she angled her mount through the trees towards the cabin, Della picked out the sound of gunshots. Her first intuitive thought was that Corby had sent some of his men to finish the job the bounty hunters had tried to do. She moved cautiously through the trees, her hand close to the Winchester. Then she relaxed as she saw that it was Mark, still practising.

He flashed her a quick smile and holstered the guns as she walked her mount along the ledge. Her grandfather was seated in one of the chairs outside, watching Mark's every move, occasionally nodding in satisfied approval.

'Did you find out anythin' in town?' Mark asked as she dismounted.

Nodding, she said, 'Like I figured, Ed Clayton seems to know quite a lot though I'm not quite sure what it means.'

'Guess we'd better hear it and then we'll decide what to do next,' Calhoun said.

Briefly, but omitting nothing, Della told them everything that Clayton had said. As she spoke, she noticed Mark's face hardening and could guess at the thoughts going through his mind.

'So Corby has moved cattle onto my spread,' he grated finally, 'and the law has done nothin' to stop him.'

Calhoun lit a smoke. He said quietly, 'There ain't much McKinrick can do. Corby is the only law in Henders Rock. The sheriff does just as he's told.'

'Then what do we do, just sit here like rats while Corby takes over everythin'?'

Calhoun gave a faint smile. 'When you get to be as old as I am, and you want to go on livin', you stop and think things out. Right now, I'm puzzled as to why this circuit judge is comin' into town. He's got somethin' in mind and I wish I knew what it was.' He flicked his glance towards Mark. 'You know anythin' about this Judge Torbin?'

Mark thought back and then nodded. 'I know the name but it's from a long time ago. I recall he was a federal marshal then, a good friend of our family.'

'So he'd know that your father had this aversion to guns?'

'I guess so. Is that important?'

Calhoun drew deeply on his cigarette. 'It could be. If he knew you'd never handled a gun in your life he might start to question this story of you shootin' a man in the back that Corby's spreadin' around. If word has reached him about your family, he might also want to ask some questions about that.'

'Corby can't allow that to happen,' Della put in.

Calhoun nodded. He rubbed his shoulder, gritting his teeth as a spasm of pain lanced through him. 'Then there's only one thing he can do. He has to make sure that Judge Torbin never gets here.'

'From what Ed Clayton said, he means to have the judge killed, Mark,' Della said gravely.

Mark thought about that and the more he turned it over in his mind, the more sense it made. Corby would stop at nothing to maintain his stranglehold on Henders Rock. Anyone who stood in his way would have to be eliminated.

'Did Clayton tell you anythin' else, Della?' Mark asked tautly.

He saw the girl hesitate as if unsure what his reaction would be. Then she said slowly, 'He told me to tell you that a Mexican called Pedro and three other strangers had been in the saloon on a number of occasions over the last few days.'

Through clenched teeth, Mark gritted, 'So they've finally decided to show themselves. Corby must feel pretty sure of himself.'

Calhoun tossed the butt of his cigarette away. Leaning back into a more comfortable position in the chair, he said somberly, 'Either they reckon you've ridden out and won't cause any more trouble, Mark, or they think you're still that greenhorn farmer and they've nothin' to worry about if you should come back lookin' for revenge.'

'Then they'll soon learn differently.' Mark's right hand touched the butt of the Colt at his hip.

'You're not thinking of riding in and taking on all four of them.' Della's face registered a look of alarm.

Meeting her direct stare, he said grimly. 'That'll come – and soon. Right now, I've got more important things to do. Somehow, I have to find out which stage Judge Torbin will be travellin' on from Twin Springs. Somehow, we've got to stop Corby from killin' him. There's only one man in Henders Rock who might tell me – Sheriff McKinrick.'

'And if you should meet up with any o' these men who killed your folks?' Calhoun asked.

'Then I'll do what I must.'

'I guess that's the way it has to be.' Calhoun sighed audibly. 'If I hadn't collected this damned slug I'd ride in with you.'

'I know that,' Mark replied. 'But—'

He broke off as Della cut in, 'I'll ride in with you, Mark. If there is any trouble, I can handle a Winchester as well as you can use those Colts.'

Mark's lips twisted into a grim smile but there was no mirth in it. 'I guess you can, Della, but this is somethin' I have to do alone.'

The girl made to protest but her grandfather butted in. 'Let him go, Della. I've taught him all I know and I figure he can now use those guns as well as I ever could.'

Mark waited until darkness was closing in before setting his mount to the steep downgrade among the firs. There was a storm brewing towards the north-west with broad thunderheads climbing high into the heavens, blotting out the last vestiges of sunset.

Eyeing them, he knew it was going to be a wet ride before he reached town. It would, however, give him the advantage that it would keep most of the townsfolk off the streets. Soon the wind got up, gusting viciously, bringing the rain with it. Large, heavy drops slashed at his face, running off the brim of his hat.

Lightning cracked like a whip above the higher ground followed by deep thunder-rolls as the storm came closer. By the time he spotted the lights of the town he was soaked to the skin.

As he had anticipated, the boardwalks were deserted. A piano was being played in the saloon and light spilled out into the street. Tethering his mount in the small alley a short distance from the saloon, Mark eased the Colts slightly in their holsters; then made to step down off the-boardwalk. The next second, he thrust himself back into the rain-dripping shadows.

McKinrick came walking slowly along the opposite boardwalk. For a moment, the sheriff paused to light a cigarette. Then he pushed open the doors and went inside. A couple of men came out and moved away, swaying slightly from side to side.

Mark waited for a couple of minutes; then crossed over to the saloon, glancing swiftly inside over the doors. The room was full with most of the tables occupied. He spotted the sheriff immediately standing at the bar in conversation with the bartender.

Pushing the door open with the flat of his hand, he went in. Going up to the bar, he stood a few feet from McKinrick and motioned to the barkeep, noticing the look of apprehension on the man's face as he came forward.

Keeping his voice down, the bartender whispered, 'What the hell are you doin' in here, Mark? I thought you'd seen sense and ridden out for good.'

Watching the other's face, Mark saw the man's glance shift suddenly towards the far end of the counter. Following his look, Mark felt himself tighten as he recognized the two men standing there. One was the Mexican, Pedro. His companion was also one of the men he had seen at the farm.

'Don't be a fool and try anythin'. Those two are poison. They'll kill you for sure.'

From the corner of his eye, Mark saw McKinrick turn, saw the startled look on the lawman's grizzled features.

'Guess you're surprised to see me, Sheriff,' he said quietly. 'Seems everyone in town figured I'd run with my tail between my legs.'

McKinrick ran his tongue around his lips. 'Better get out o' here while you still can, Mark. I don't want any trouble and I sure don't want to see you carried out to the morgue.'

'It was you I came to see, Sheriff, but it seems you're now lettin' Corby's murderin' skunks walk freely around town.'

'Now see here, Mark. If you're meanin' Dominguez and Kender at the bar yonder, I got no—'

Before he could complete his sentence, a sudden shout came from along the counter, rising above the background noise. Pedro stepped away from the bar. He was staring in Mark's direction and there was a sneering grin on his sallow features.

Pushing his hat back on his head, he stepped away from the counter. Behind him, Kender turned and then moved away towards the middle of the floor.

'Well now, if it isn't the farmer boy,' Pedro sniggered contemptuously. 'And he's wearin' guns.'

'Which is more than any of my family were when you shot them down in cold blood,' Mark said icily. A sudden calm had now settled over him as he eyed the two men. He recognized that the other was deliberately trying to rile him, force him into a rash act. Unfocusing his gaze as Calhoun had taught him, he moved away from the counter, watching both men closely.

'Reckon it's time he was taught a lesson,' Kender said maliciously. 'One he ain't goin' to forget in a hurry.'

'Now just simmer down, boys,' McKinrick said hastily. 'Kennick here is a wanted man and I intend to lock him in jail until the circuit judge gets here. There ain't no call for gunplay.'

'You stay out o' this, lawman,' Pedro gritted harshly. 'We just heard him accuse us o' killin' his family and in front of all these folk here. Now that's somethin' we don't take from any two-bit tinhorn.'

'So what are you goin' to do about it?' Holding his hands by his sides, Mark kept both men in focus. 'It seems to me that all you can do is talk.'

A surge of fury flashed across the Mexican's face at this implied insult. He made to turn towards his companion and as if this had been a pre-arranged signal, both men went for their guns.

Mark's hands seemed to move of their own volition. Almost before he was aware of it the Colts were in his hands, his fingers squeezing the triggers simultaneously. Pedro's gun was just clear of leather when the slug took him high in the chest. The impact drove him back into one of the tables as he went down.

Three feet away, his companion was teetering on his feet. The Colt in his hand roared once, the bullet ploughing a neat furrow into the floor at his feet. For a moment, he stared directly at Mark. Then all of the starch went out of him as his legs buckled. The nearby table overturned sending glasses onto the floor.

'Anyone else want to go the same way?' Mark swung the Colts in wide arcs covering everyone in the saloon. When no one made a move, he turned to face the sheriff.

'I don't want to have to kill you, Sheriff,' he said thinly. 'But I don't intend to spend any time in one o' your cells. All I need from you is some information.'

McKinrick's face was twisted into a mask of utter consternation at what he had just witnessed. 'You . . . you just outdrew and shot down two of Corby's best gunslingers.' he gasped. 'I wouldn't have believed it if I hadn't seen it. How the hell did you—?'

'Let's just say I had a good teacher,' Mark replied coldly. 'Now just step outside.' He motioned with one of the Colts towards the door to emphasize his order.

As the sheriff moved away from the bar, Mark let his glance rove over the men seated at the tables. It was evident from their dumbfounded attitudes that this was something they had not expected. Very quietly, he said, 'Just remain where you are – all o' you. I ain't gone yet and the first man to step through that door gets a bullet in him.'

'Now you're talkin' just like Calhoun,' McKinrick muttered. Keeping his hands well away from his sides, he walked to the door, pushed it open and stepped out onto the boardwalk.

Mark pushed one of the Colts back into its holster, keeping the lawman covered with the other. There were several horses tethered to the hitching rail. Loosening the reins of the nearest, he slapped it hard on the rump sending it racing towards the south end of the street.

Prodding McKinrick in the back, he thrust him across the street and into the narrow alley. Less than ten seconds later, the doors of the saloon swung open and several men came running through, glancing up and down the street.

One of the men pointed as he yelled, 'There he goes! That's his mount.'

Mounting up quickly, the riders spurred after the running stallion. Smiling grimly, Mark turned back to the sheriff. 'By the time they catch up with that riderless horse, I'll be gone.'

'A neat trick,' the sheriff said grudgingly. 'But you won't last long once Corby hears o' this. I tried to warn you against Corby when you first rode into town but now you're just as much an outlaw as that man you're ridin' with.'

'Circumstances have a habit of changing men,'

Mark remarked grimly. 'Now, all I want to know is when Judge Torbin is comin' on that stage from Twin Springs.'

The sheriff evinced surprise. 'How did you get to know about that? I only found out myself a couple o' days ago. You aimin' to kill him too?'

'I aim to save his life. But someone in town is determined to stop him; someone who's already figured that Torbin might start askin' awkward questions about who gave the orders for my family to be killed – and why?'

'You still accusin' Seth Corby?'

'Who else? Those two men I just killed in there were with that party who raided the farm. I saw them there and I'll never forget their faces. Now – are you goin' to answer my question?'

The sheriff remained silent for so long that Mark thought he did not intend to answer him. Then he said tightly, 'Somehow, I've got the feelin' that you're on the level about this, Mark. As a lawman I don't approve of the way you're goin' about it. All right, I'll tell you. Judge Torbin is takin' the stage from Twin Springs next Wednesday.'

'Thanks, Sheriff. That's all I wanted to know. Just one other thing – not a word o' this to Corby.'

'And those two remainin' men who shot up your family – what about them?'

Mark's answering smile was not a nice thing. 'I'll deal with 'em later if they're still around. If not, I'll hunt them down, you can be sure of that.'

The cold and dispassionate way Mark made the threat sent a shiver along McKinrick's spine. He stood in silence as the other swung into the saddle and rode swiftly along the alley into the rain-dripping darkness.

CHAPTER VI

TREACHERY!

From among the high bluffs, the narrow trail from Twin Springs was a pale ribbon scarcely distinguishable from the arid land on either side. In the blazing early afternoon sun it lay empty in both directions. Heat shimmered the surface so that it appeared to be covered in a layer of rippling water.

The two men who sat their mounts in the long shadow of a tall butte had ridden hard for the past three hours, skirting around Henders Rock and keeping the trail in full sight most of the way.

Taking a half-smoked cigarette from between his lips, Mark asked, 'How do you figure Corby is goin' to do this, Frank?'

Calhoun turned slightly in the saddle, squinting into the sun beneath lowered lids. 'Knowin' him, he'll send a bunch of his hired gunhawks with orders to kill everyone on board the stage. He certainly won't want to leave any witnesses.'

Rubbing a hand down his cheek where the itching dust had worked its way into the folds of his skin, Mark pondered on that. While it would be the simplest and most logical way to ensure Torbin never reached his destination, there was a nagging little suspicion at the back of his mind.

If the rancher did it that way there were a number of things that could go wrong and Corby was not a man to take any chances. There would undoubtedly be an armed guard riding with the stage. Furthermore, having once been a federal marshal, Torbin knew how to use a gun and Corby might lose several men in the hold-up. In addition there were only a few places along this trail where a bunch of men might lie in concealment, all places well known to the men who drove and guarded the stage.

'Something botherin' you, Mark?' Calhoun asked the question without taking his eyes off the empty trail.

'Just tryin' to put myself in Corby's position, Frank. He's a careful man and you can be sure he's thought all of this out, down to the last detail. I've got the feelin' in my bones he has another ace up his sleeve but I can't figure out what it is.'

Half an hour earlier at the stage depot in Twin Springs, Sam Wellard stood on the boardwalk, acutely aware of the man who stood just a couple of feet behind him. They had both ridden in together that morning, leaving Henders Rock just before daybreak.

It wasn't the thought of killing this circuit judge

that bothered him. In the past he had killed several men, very few of them in fair fight. What worried him was this man Corson who had accompanied him on Corby's orders. Once he had carried out his part of the bargain and killed Torbin what guarantee did he have that a mount and that $5,000 would be there?

It seemed more likely that Corson had orders to kill him and the knowledge that there would be a gun trained on him while they were on the stage, making sure he did exactly as he had been told, made him doubly nervous.

Four other people were waiting for the stage. One of them was a tall, grey-haired man in his sixties with a gunbelt strapped to his waist. He guessed that this was Judge Torbin, the man he had to kill.

Five minutes later, the stage came into sight around the corner and drew up in front of them. A whiskered oldster sat on the board beside the driver. He had a rifle in his hands and in spite of his age, Wellard reckoned he knew how to use it.

Seating himself opposite Torbin, Wellard settled back as Corson crushed into the seat beside him. He felt tensed and nervous as he studied the other passengers. Two women, evidently mother and daughter sat across from each other at the opposite door. The sixth was a short, flashily dressed man with a diamond tie pin showing plainly above his waistcoat. Clearly a gambler or a banker, Wellard decided.

Once the action began, he doubted if there would be any trouble from them. Torbin, however, was a different matter. The first sign of any trouble and those Colts would be in his hands and then all hell

112

could break loose.

Moistening his dry lips, he leaned his shoulders against the seat and forced himself to relax. With Corson seated beside him, his hand never very far from the gun at his waist, there was nothing he could do but go through with this. His only hope was that Corby was a man of his word and there would be that mount and money waiting for him.

Inside the stage the heat began to rise. Once they left the outskirts of Twin Springs it would get worse as they headed into the drylands. Taking out his handkerchief, Wellard mopped his face aware that Corson was watching his every move.

'Any of you gentlemen goin' far?' Torbin leaned forward slightly, his keen gaze flicking from one man to the other.

Wellard shook his head and forced evenness into his voice as he replied, 'Only as far as Henders Rock.'

Torbin pursed his lips into a hard line. 'I've heard there's been some trouble there recently. Some family killed and their house burned.'

Beside Wellard, Corson shrugged negligently. 'These things happen all the time. Henders Rock is a frontier town, no worse than any others in this territory.'

'Doesn't the law do anythin' about it?' demanded the older woman. 'I thought they had a sheriff there to put a stop to such things.'

'Perhaps the sheriff isn't the real law in that town,' Torbin commented. 'If the townsfolk won't back him in a showdown you'll often find that some big landowner is the one who makes the laws. Whenever that happens someone from outside has to go in and impose some kind of order.' He looked directly at Corson as he spoke.

'And you intend to do that, Judge?' Wellard said.

The other gave a grim smile. 'I see you know who I am.'

'Sure. You're the circuit judge for this territory.'

Through tight lips, Corson said tautly, 'If that's what you're aimin' to do, I reckon you won't find it as easy as you think. Seth Corby owns most o' the land there, all bought and paid for. He ain't the kind o' man to take orders from anyone – not even circuit judges.'

'Then I guess we'll have to see about that when I get there,' Torbin remarked drily.

The stage had now left Twin Springs behind and the trail became more rocky and uneven, jolting the passengers around. Without appearing conspicuous, Corson was watching the terrain through the window. Pressing his face close to the glass, Wellard narrowed his eyes against the harsh sunlight and tried to make out details.

Corby had been quite specific about where they were to stop the coach. Up ahead, about a mile away, he could just make out where the trail curved to their left. Tall buttes stood on either side, narrowing the track considerably.

Tensing himself, he waited for Corson to make the first move, knowing that when he did he would have to move quickly.

Five minutes later, the gunman pushed himself to his feet, jerking the Colt from its holster in the same movement. At the same moment, Wellard drew his gun, levelling it on Torbin. 'Unbuckle that gunbelt, Judge, and pass it to me. Do it slowly and no tricks or my friend will shoot these passengers, one at a time.'

'You won't get away with holdin' up the stage like this,' Torbin said harshly. 'We're not carryin' any gold.'

'We know that,' Corson snapped. 'We're not after gold: it's you we want.'

Very slowly, Torbin unbuckled the gunbelt and pulled it from around his waist. For a moment, he seemed on the point of swinging it at the gun in Wellard's hand, then thought better of it.

Taking it from him, Wellard lowered the window and tossed it out. Beside him, Corson tilted the Colt in his hand and fired a couple of shots through the roof. There came a harsh grunt and a moment later, the body of the guard fell past the far window.

Corson called loudly, 'Stop this coach, driver, or the next bullet is for you.'

Near the window, the older woman uttered a thin scream. Above it, Wellard heard the sound of the handbrake being applied as the driver reined hard on the horses. Slowly, the stage ground to a halt.

Thrusting the door open, Wellard stepped out, keeping his Colt trained on the judge. Behind Torbin, Corson rammed the barrel of his weapon hard into the judge's back. 'Get out, Torbin,' he ordered harshly.

When the three of them were standing by the side of the trail, Corson slammed the coach door shut and moved away. Glancing up at the driver, he said,

'You can be on your way now. We've got what we want.'

The driver stared down at him and then lifted the whip, bringing it down on the horses' backs scarcely able to believe that they were free to continue their journey. Corson watched until the stage was little more than a dot shrouded in white dust.

Turning to Torbin he said thinly, 'All right, Judge. The three of us are goin' to take a little walk behind this butte. As I reckon you've already guessed, only two of us are comin' back.'

'You think that by killin' me you'll stop the law getting' into that helltown? That place will be swarmin' with federal marshals the minute this gets out.'

Corson grind viciously. 'I reckon by that time, Mr Corby will have brought in so many men they'll not be able to do a thing about it. Now get moving.'

From among the buttes, Mark and Calhoun had seen the stage approaching at a rapid pace dragging a trail of white dust behind it. Throwing a quick glance in the other direction, Frank said tautly, 'If any o' Corby's men are out to hold up that stage, they should've been in sight by now. I'd say this is the most likely place for an attack yet there's no sign of 'em.'

'Unless one or more of his men are already on it,' Mark muttered harshly. He wheeled his mount and made to put it to the downgrade just as the coach drew level with them and two shots rang out.

Some twenty feet below them, they saw the guard suddenly reel, the rifle falling from his hands as the slugs took him in the back. His body arched; then toppled sideways, pitching him into the dust.

'Goddamnit! You're right.' Calhoun snapped.

Mark caught at the other's reins. 'Hold hard, Frank. There must be other passengers in that coach.'

They watched as the stage slowed to a halt. The far door opened and three men got out. Mark instantly recognized the tall man, grey hair showing beneath his hat. 'That's Judge Torbin.'

'Then the other two must be workin' for Corby. I reckon they intend to kill him here and probably bury him in the alkali. Not even the coyotes will find him if they do that.'

A few moments later they heard a shout and the coach moved off. Now they were able to see the three figures plainly. Thinly, Frank said, 'That man down there is one o' those bounty hunters. I'd know him anywhere. Reckon he's thrown in his lot with Corby.'

The trio passed out of sight around the edge of the butte. No sooner had they done so than Mark and Calhoun put their mounts to the steep downgrade. The horses made no sound in the soft alkali. Slipping from the saddle on the run, Mark drew one of the Colts and edged along the high wall of rock with Calhoun close on his heels.

The sound of harsh voices reached them a few moments later. Close to Mark's head was a narrow crack in the rock. Pressing himself hard against it, he managed to glimpse the men some ten yards away.

The gunman was saying, 'Reckon this is where your career comes to an end, Torbin. My friend here

117

reckons he's been paid five thousand dollars to kill you.' Turning swiftly from the hip, he levelled his Colt at the bounty hunter. 'Drop that gun, Wellard. This money Corby gave me to pay you off will see me clear across the border on that mount yonder.'

For a moment, Wellard seemed on the point of making his play, then let the Colt fall to the ground at his feet.

'That's better.' Corson grinned. 'If either o' you have any prayers to say, I reckon you'd better say 'em now.'

'I should've known the kind o' lowdown snake you are, Corson,' he grated thinly. 'I ought to have shot you before.'

'That was your mistake, Wellard. Now you're goin' to pay for it.'

Mark didn't wait a moment longer. Stepping out from around the rock, he said crisply, 'Don't be too sure o' that, friend.'

Corson swung round, a grimace of astonishment on his swarthy features. Swiftly, he brought up his gun, finger tight on the trigger. The two shots blurred into one, sending echoes chasing themselves among the buttes.

Mark felt the scorching sting of a bullet past his cheek. Corson slowly twisted at the waist, struggling desperately to get off another shot. Then his knees bent as he dropped at Wellard's feet.

Even as the gunslinger fell, Wellard dived for the gun he had dropped. Closing his fingers around it, he straightened, his lips drawn back over his teeth. The Colt in Calhoun's fist spoke once and the bounty hunter staggered back, one hand clutching at his chest.

Going forward, Mark said, 'I reckon we got here just in time, Judge. We guessed Corby would do something to stop you gettin' to Henders Rock.'

'But the way we figured it, he'd send a bunch of his men to hold up the stage,' Calhoun put in.

Giving a nod, Torbin glanced from one man to the other, finally resting on Mark. 'You're Jed Kennick's son, aren't you?'

'That's right. I'm sure it was Corby who sent five gunslingers to murder my family but so far I've got no proof o' that.'

'And wearin' guns. I wonder what your pa would say to that if he were alive.'

Grimly, Mark said, 'I made a promise to him just before he died. I swore I'd get those responsible and I still aim to do that. Three o' those murderers are dead now.'

'And you're still fixin' to get the other two? Well, I can't say I blame you. A man has a right to justice and it sometimes has to be done with a gun.

'And you don't have to tell me who you are,' Torbin went on, glancing at Mark's companion. 'I've seen your face a dozen times in a dozen different places. Frank Calhoun. Yet it seems I owe my life to both of you.'

'Frank saved my life and also taught me how to use these Colts. I guess if it weren't for him, I'd also be dead by now.'

Calhoun gestured towards the waiting horse. 'I suggest you take that bronc, Judge and we'll ride back with you to Henders Rock. Neither o' these two critters will be needin' it now.'

Going forward, Mark felt inside Corson's shirt pocket and took out a small envelope. He handed it to Torbin. 'I think you'll find quite a heap o' dollars in there, Judge. It's blood money Corby paid to have you eliminated.'

'Thanks.' Torbin thrust it into his pocket, then caught the bridle of the waiting horse, leading it back to the trail. Picking up the gunbelt which Wellard had thrown from the stage, Torbin buckled it around his waist before climbing into the saddle.

Riding between Mark and Calhoun, Torbin said, 'What do you know about the sheriff in Henders Rock? Can he be trusted or is he in cahoots with this rancher Corby?'

Mark thought for a moment before answering. 'I guess he's straight, but he's an old man. Corby just keeps him in that job because he does as he's told. The first time he gets out o' line, Corby will put one of his own men in as sheriff and McKinrick knows it.'

'So it's Corby who runs the town?'

'Yeah. That's why I'm not so sure if it would be wise for you to ride in openly. He's made one try to get you killed. You can be sure he'll try again.'

'Then what do you suggest?'

'At the moment, Corby reckons you're dead. If we're lucky, he'll figure that those two split the money between 'em and lit out for the border. In the meantime, you might be a lot safer if you were to come with us.'

For an instant, an expression of suspicion flashed

across Torbin's bluff features but it was gone in a moment. 'And where might that be?'

'A little shack I've got up in the hills,' Calhoun replied. 'We should be safe there for a little while but if that *hombre* Wellard has informed Corby of our whereabouts he might send a band of his men up there, particularly if he should learn that you're still alive.'

'Very well.' Torbin nodded in acquiescence. 'We go there. It seems I need a lot of information about what's goin' on in Henders Rock.'

As they rode into the clearing, Della appeared in the doorway holding a rifle in her hands. She lowered it as she came towards them, glancing up at the man who rode with them.

'This is Circuit Judge Torbin,' her grandfather explained. 'As we figured an attempt was made to kill him before he got to town. The last o' those bounty hunters is dead together with one o' Corby's men.'

Della gave Torbin a warm smile as she led him into the cabin. 'I've no doubt my grandfather and Mark have told you something of what's been happening around here,' she said, motioning him to a chair.

Sinking into it, Torbin nodded. 'I've learned some of it,' he replied, 'but there's a lot more I need to know, especially about this man Corby. From what little I know, it seems he's been takin' over peoples' land either by force or buyin' them out at far less than their spreads are worth.'

'Any who've tried to stand up to him have been killed,' Mark interposed. 'I know that only too well.'

121

Going to the small cupboard, Calhoun brought out a bottle of whiskey and glasses, setting them on the table. 'Have some o' this, Judge,' he said. 'It'll wash some o' that alkali from our throats.'

After taking a couple of sips, Torbin said, 'It seems to me you have a big problem here. This man is runnin' the town and has the men to back his play. Won't any o' the townsfolk make a stand?'

Mark shook his head. 'They're too scared. They don't like him but you can't expect ordinary folk to go against seasoned gunfighters. I reckon Corby has at least thirty men on his payroll and he can probably bring in more at a moment's notice.'

A grim smile twitched the judge's lips. 'So what do you reckon the three o' you can do? You need men with guns behind you if you're ever to bring any kind o' law and order to this helltown.'

Rubbing his bandaged shoulder where the ache still persisted, Calhoun lowered himself into a chair. 'I've seen a lot o' towns like this along the frontier,' he said solemnly. 'Either they tear themselves to pieces in a range war – or somehow they make a stand and say enough is enough. If they make a stand then that town will grow but if not it'll just vanish off the map.'

Torbin stared at him over the rim of his glass. 'When you talk like that, Calhoun, it's hard to believe you're a wanted outlaw.'

Mark saw Della's face harden. 'My grandfather is no outlaw, Judge Torbin. It's very easy for men to give that name to anyone. Just because he went out to avenge his family, the law in this town, Corby's law, has declared that Mark is an outlaw.'

'I get your point, Della,' Torbin said calmly. He finished his drink and took out a cigar, lighting it and blowing a cloud of smoke towards the ceiling. 'Right now, however, there are more important matters we have to talk about. I could bring in a couple o' federal marshals, but my guess is that Corby is far too smart to leave any evidence around which might prove he's broken the law.'

'There's just one chance – a slim one but it might work.'

'Then let's hear it,' Della said.

'Most o' those smaller ranchers who were forced off their spreads by Corby left the territory. But there are still a few of 'em around – bitter, angry men who might want to see Corby finished. In the past the law did nothin' to help them. But if we could get them together and you could talk to them, Judge, they might back us.'

Torbin mused on that for a few moments; then said, 'It might help talkin' to them. But how many of them are there? Not many, I guess. You need men to back you in this, plenty o' men.'

'They must have had men workin' for them when they owned their own spreads,' Della interjected. 'If they were able to hire them then, it's possible they could do so now.'

'But it would have to be done without Corby getting wind of it,' Mark cautioned, 'otherwise he could hit them one at a time before they banded together.'

Torbin fished inside his pocket and brought out

the small envelope. 'Maybe this ain't strictly accordin' to the law,' he said with a strange glint in his eyes, 'but since Corby evidently paid this to have me killed, I reckon we can put it to good use.'

'In what way?' Della asked.

'Well to my way o' thinking, if these men you mention are to bring in more gunmen to help us against Corby, they'll have to be paid. I reckon this should help.'

'There's one other problem we have to be prepared for,' Calhoun put in. 'Very soon Corby will know you're still alive and he won't be sittin' still allowin' events to take their own course.'

'Meaning?'

'Meanin' that we can't stay here. He has enough hired gunhawks to wipe us all out. My guess is that he's already getting his men together to hit this place within the next few hours.'

'Do you know of any other place where we might hide out?' Torbin asked tautly.

'There's an old adobe village about ten miles across the desert yonder,' Calhoun said after a reflective pause. 'We could make it in a couple of hours, but I suggest we wait until dark just in case Corby has any men scouring the area for us.'

'Then that's what we'll do,' Torbin agreed. 'We'd better take some supplies with us. There's no tellin' how long we'll have to stay there.'

Seth Corby was standing just outside the sheriff's office with McKinrick beside him when the stage rolled into town. One glance was sufficient to tell

McKinrick that something had happened. There was no sign of the usual guard and one of the windows had been smashed with shards of broken glass still glittering around the edges.

He went forward quickly, glancing up at the driver. 'What the hell happened, Clem?' he called loudly. 'A hold-up?' It was the only thing he could think of.

'You might call it that, Sheriff.' The driver got down and opened the door allowing the passengers to alight. 'Some *hombre* inside the coach fired through the roof, hitting Seddon in the back. He's lyin' back along the trail somewhere.'

'What was it – a robbery?' Corby asked loudly. Inwardly, he knew the answer and a sense of elation filled him. Evidently those two men had done exactly what he had told them. Whatever happened however, he must not give himself away.

Clem shook his head. 'Weren't nothin' like that. There were two of 'em working together. They took one o' the passengers off the coach into the rocks, lettin' the rest of us go. I figure they meant to kill him.'

McKinrick's glance passed over those who had stepped down from the coach. He felt a sudden shocked sensation in the pit of his stomach. Judge Torbin was not among them.

Turning to him, Corby said sharply, 'You know who this man was those gunmen took off the stage?'

'Judge Torbin was travellin' on it today from Twin Springs. I got word from him a couple o' days ago. He ain't here so I guess it must've been him.'

Corby feigned a look of stunned shock and

surprise. 'You're sayin' that someone has killed the circuit judge? But who'd want to do that?'

'Someone who didn't want him to reach Henders Rock, I guess,' declared the driver. 'There weren't no doubt they knew exactly who he was. This must've been planned before we left Twin Springs.'

'Then I reckon it's your duty to look into this and bring these killers to justice, Sheriff,' Corby said harshly. 'If you need any o' my men to help you hunt 'em down, you can have 'em.'

'There's no call for that at the moment,' McKinrick grunted. 'I can get a posse together and we'll ride out along the trail and see what we can find.'

'Then I suggest you do that right away, otherwise these killers could be well over the border by the time you have your men ready.' Corby spun on his heel and left. There was a feeling of intense satisfaction in his mind as he entered the saloon.

With Torbin out of the way and nothing to connect him with the judge's murder, his only concern now was with Kennick and that outlaw he was running with. Not that he anticipated much trouble with either of them. Certainly he hadn't got his hands on those land deeds but with his cattle now roaming that farmland, there was nothing Kennick could do.

Fifteen minutes later, McKinrick rode out of Henders Rock with twelve men at his back. Torbin's death had shocked him. Inwardly, he was asking himself how many folk in town knew that the judge would be riding that stage. Certainly someone apart from himself had prior knowledge of it since everything about the affair seemed to have been meticulously planned to the last detail.

He knew that once word of it got back to Twin Springs there would be men in Henders Rock asking a lot of questions, most of them directed at himself. It was possible that Corby, in spite of his outward appearance of shocked surprise, had had a hand in it.

On the other hand, there were sure to be a number of people who had a grudge against Torbin. In his career as circuit judge he had undoubtedly had several men hanged and there were always some who might hate him sufficiently to want him dead.

Sighing, he forced himself to concentrate on the job in hand, letting his glance rove over both sides of the trail.

Half an hour later, they spotted the body lying in the middle of the track. Swinging from the saddle he ran forward, bending to turn the man over. 'Shot in the back,' he said as the rest of the men came up. 'He must have been the guard they killed.'

Getting to his feet, he ordered, 'Search both sides of the trail. If Judge Torbin is dead, his body will be somewhere close by.'

The posse spread out, moving around the surrounding buttes. A few moments later, a shout rang out. 'Over here, Sheriff. There are a couple o' bodies lyin' here. They've both been shot.'

Two bodies? McKinrick thought as he moved towards the towering butte. Had Torbin managed to kill one of his attackers before he himself had been killed? Moving as quickly as possible, he found the posse man bending over the bodies.

His feeling of apprehension changed to one of astonishment. Neither of the men was Torbin. He recognized the man in the frock coat as one of the four bounty hunters who had ridden into town some days earlier on the trail of Frank Calhoun. The second man seemed to be a common gunslinger.

His face a mask of mixed emotions, he stared round at the men with him. 'If Torbin was taken off that stage at gunpoint, how the hell did he manage to kill 'em both? And where the hell is he now?'

One of the men moved away a short distance. 'There are hoofmarks here, Sheriff.' He turned and stared off into the distance. 'But there are none headin' out that way into the badlands. Whoever took it went back onto the trail yonder.'

'There are more here,' called a second man. 'I'd say at least two sets. My guess is there were at least two more men here apart from the other three.'

McKinrick ran his hand over the stubble on his chin. 'This don't make any sense.' He muttered finally. 'Why would two men just happen to be here, rescue Torbin from these killers, and then make off with him?'

'Beats me,' grunted the first man. 'I doubt if we'll find any evidence on the trail to tell us which way they went. The ground is too hard there to leave any marks.'

'So all we know is that whoever attempted to kill Torbin didn't succeed and the possibility is that he's still alive somewhere in the territory,' the sheriff conceded. 'Let's get these bodies back to town. We won't find much more here.'

All the way back into town, McKinrick tried to figure out what had happened after Torbin had been taken off the stage. Someone wanted the circuit judge killed and had laid careful plans for it to be achieved. Yet someone else had evidently saved his life – but for what purpose, he couldn't determine.

He half-expected to find Torbin waiting for him when he got back into town but, after depositing the three bodies at the mortuary, he checked the hotel but it soon became clear that the judge was nowhere in town.

Going into the saloon, he noticed Corby sitting with his three acquaintances playing poker at one of the tables. Stepping up to the bar, he asked the bartender for whiskey. Through the mirror at the rear he saw Corby say something to the men sitting with him. The rancher rose swiftly to his feet and moved across to him, resting his elbows on the bar.

'Have that drink on me, Sheriff,' Corby said cordially. 'You look as though you've had a long and dusty ride. You find anything?'

McKinrick nodded, took off his hat and laid it on the counter in front of him. 'We came across three bodies along the trail,' he said, pouring the whiskey into his glass.

'Three bodies?' For a moment, something like surprise showed on the other's face but he quickly controlled himself.

'That's right. One was the guard, shot twice in the back. Of the other two, I only recognized one.'

'Oh, who was he?' Corby tried to make his voice sound casual.

'He was one o' those four bounty hunters. The other *hombre* was a stranger to me. Looked like some hired killer from outside the territory. There was no sign o' the circuit judge.' Turning his head, the sheriff stared directly into Corby's eyes. 'Now to me that seems mighty peculiar.'

'In what way, Sheriff?' Corby tried to suppress his fury and bewilderment.

'Well, we've got the statement o' the stage driver who claims Torbin was taken away at gunpoint by these two men. So how the hell did he not only get away but manage to shoot those two men?'

Corby shrugged. 'Your guess is as good as mine, McKinrick.' He finished his drink and then went out, ignoring the three men at the card table who waved him over. He was in no mood for poker tonight. Something had happened out there on the trail. Those two men he had sent out to kill Torbin had fouled up.

The outcome of it was that the circuit judge was still alive and if he wasn't in town, whoever had saved him clearly had him stashed away somewhere. His thoughts instantly jumped to Mark Kennick. Someone had taught that farmer's boy how to use a gun. From what he had been told, Kennick had outdrawn and killed Pedro and Kender in the saloon.

Now that he was thinking clearly and coherently, he recalled how Jed had been killed when he had taunted Kennick into a gunfight. Only one man

130

could have turned the farmer boy into a seasoned gunfighter – Frank Calhoun!

Somehow, those two had learned that Torbin would be on that stage. How they had known he planned to have him killed was something he didn't know. Tightening the cinch beneath his mount's belly, he swung into the saddle and rode back swiftly to the ranch.

Events were now getting out of hand, he thought savagely. If he was thinking right, then Torbin was with Kennick and Calhoun. It was the only conclusion that made any sense. For a moment, his fury threatened to consume him. Once again, those two had forestalled him. Then he forced himself to calm down. At least he had a good idea where they were.

Grinning wolfishly, he rode into the courtyard. Calling harshly to Cranton, his foreman, he gave him orders to collect as many men as possible and be ready to ride out once it was dark. This time there would be no mistake.

The moon was just lifting above the trees when Calhoun closed the door of the cabin. The others were already in the saddle, waiting for him. Leaving the heights, they moved down the rugged slopes to where the flat, arid land glowed faintly in the pale wash of moonlight a couple of hundred feet below them.

Here there were no trails and they had to pick their way carefully through the firs. At times, they were forced to halt while Calhoun moved slowly ahead, looking for a way down.

Half an hour passed before they reached the bottom. In front of them was nothing but white alkali and a few stunted bushes. Before they set out to cross it, Calhoun directed each of them to cut a long branch from the trees.

'If Corby and his men do come and find nobody here, we don't want him pickin' up our trail across this alkali,' he explained. 'This is an old Indian trick I learned when I spent some time with the Sioux. We all drag one o' these behind us and it'll cover our tracks.'

In a tight bunch, they set out across the badlands, the branches obliterating all evidence of hoofmarks at their backs. By the time they came within sight of the small Indian village the moon was high in the cloudless heavens.

The small buildings were arranged in a circle, standing silently in the flooding moonlight. Long black shadows lay among them. Riding in the lead with Calhoun, Mark ran his keen gaze over the dark shadows. The place seemed too quiet and the small hairs on the back of his neck lifted uncomfortably.

Entering the clear space in the centre he sat tautly in the saddle unsure of what was bothering him.

'Something wrong, Mark?' Della halted her mount beside him, noticing the worried frown on his face.

'I'm not sure. It's just that—'

Before he could finish his sentence a sudden harsh shout rang out from the shadows between the houses. 'Raise your hands, all of you! Make any move for your guns and it'll be your last.'

Very slowly, Mark lifted his hands, trying to determine exactly where the voice had come from. The next moment, a dark, indistinct figure stepped into sight, a rifle in his hands. A second movement brought Mark's head round. Three more men armed with rifles came out of the shadows.

'Throw your weapons down,' snapped one of the other men, 'then get down off your mounts.'

For an instant, Mark considered going for his guns, then thought better of it. With those four rifles trained on them, they had no chance. Slowly, he unbuckled the gunbelt and let it fall into the dirt as the others did the same.

As he slid from the saddle, one of the men advanced until he was standing a couple of feet away, his finger tight on the trigger. In the brilliant moonlight, Mark saw the other's face clearly for the first time.

'Cy Roberts,' he said in bemused wonderment. 'Last I heard you'd ridden east. Don't you remember me, Mark Kennick? Your spread was close to ours before Corby drove you out.'

The other peered closely at Mark's face; then slowly lowered the rifle. 'Mark Kennick – sure I remember you but what the hell are you doin' here and who are your friends?'

'You know this man, Mark?' Della came forward as the other three men came up to them.

'Sure I know him. He was a good friend of ours. Like us, Corby ran him off his ranch and took it over for himself.' To Roberts, he said, 'This is Judge Torbin, the circuit judge and the other man there is Frank Calhoun.'

'Calhoun – the outlaw?' The other scratched his head in obvious bewilderment. 'You sure keep strange company these days.'

Roberts turned to his three companions. 'Guess you may also remember Bert Clements, Slim Johnson and Herb Forrester. Like me, they lost everythin' when that snake Corby rode roughshod over the territory.'

'That's something I aim to see put right, Roberts,' Torbin said thinly.

'Yeah – and how do you figure on doin' that, Judge?' Forrester asked. 'Corby has the upper hand now. Nobody dare go against him. He has too many men to back him. McKinrick will do nothin'.'

'No – but I intend to do somethin',' Torbin said. 'But we need your help. We hadn't figured on findin' you here but it sure simplifies things a great deal.'

'Are you all on the run from Corby?' asked Clements pointedly. 'If you are, it seems to me you're in the same boat as we are.'

Roberts silenced the other with a sharp gesture. 'Let's get these folk comfortable first.' he said thinly. 'Then we'll hear what they have to say.' He pointed to the ground, 'better pick up your weapons. When you rode in, we had you figured for some o' Corby's men. Even out here, well away from town, we can't take any chances.'

He led the way to one of the low buildings and lit a lamp. In the dim, flickering light, Mark made out a number of straw pallets laid out against the walls. There was a long table in the middle with some rickety chairs around it.

'We've got plenty o' blankets,' Forrester said. 'We daren't light a fire or the smoke might be seen for miles around. There ain't many travel this way but Corby has been known to bring in men from somewhere to the west o' here.'

'We brought some provisions with us,' Della said.

'And plenty of ammunition,' Calhoun put in grimly.

Motioning them to sit, Roberts said, 'We have plenty o' water, grub and liquor. Whenever we run short one of us rides into town. Fortunately we still have some friends there who let us have supplies and ask no questions.'

Standing by the wall near the door, Forrester asked, 'What is it you want of us? There ain't much the four of us can do to finish Corby.'

'No, but back in the old days you had plenty o' men workin' for you,' Mark said earnestly. 'Men you could still get if there's a chance you'll have your land back. Do you know if there are any others who were forced out by Corby still around Henders Rock?'

The four men thought that over, then shook their heads. 'Afraid not,' Johnson muttered. 'Those that weren't killed cut their losses and headed back East.'

'Even if we did go in with you,' Roberts said, 'how are we to pay these men? Corby cleaned us all out.'

'With this.' Torbin pulled the envelope from his pocket. 'There's five thousand dollars o' Corby's money in there – money he paid to have me killed.' He stared grimly at each of the four men in turn. 'I don't know how determined you men are to see

135

Corby in jail or run out o' the territory, but I'm willin' to trust you. There's not much time. We'll need as many men as you can get within the next couple o' days if we're to have a fightin' chance.'

Roberts picked up the envelope and took out the thick wad of bills. Then he put it back, and replaced the envelope on the table. Through tight lips, he said, 'I can't speak for the others but I'm in. All I want is to see Corby danglin' on the end of a rope.'

'I guess that goes for the rest of us,' Forrester affirmed. 'We'll get those men for you.'

'Good.' Torbin nodded. 'Get as many as you can and bring 'em back here.'

CHAPTER VII

TWISTED TRAILS

That night, twenty men rode out from the ranch with Seth Corby in the lead, meeting up with the main north trail from Henders Rock half an hour later. Corby no longer had any doubt as to where the circuit judge was at that moment. Once they had stepped in to save him, Kennick and Calhoun would head straight for their hide-out somewhere in the hills.

This time, however, they would not get away from him. By dawn, he meant to see that all of them were dead and no longer able to thwart his plans. At first, killing the circuit judge had posed a problem but now Torbin had played right into his hands.

With no one left alive to testify, he would simply say that Torbin had been taken hostage by Calhoun and he had been merely trying to free him. Unfortunately Calhoun had shot the judge in cold blood before he could prevent it.

He knew there was a distinct possibility he and his men would be seen as they crossed the plain. In the flooding yellow moonlight a bunch of riders as large as this could be spotted for miles. But unlike those bounty hunters, he had more than enough men with him to crush any resistance and once among the trees there would be plenty of cover.

Swinging off the trail they headed into the badlands. Ahead, the hills showed as a long dark shadow across the horizon. From Wellard he had gained a little information as to the exact where-abouts of this cabin where Kennick and Calhoun were holed up, sufficient to pinpoint it with a fair degree of accuracy without having to scour the whole area.

Half an hour later, they reached the lower slopes and reined up their mounts. Staring up at the dark mass of the trees, Corby tried to pick out any sign of a trail. Finally, he called, 'All of you men, move your mounts up through the trees. Watch yourselves – there may be an ambush waitin' for us.'

Grumbling a little among themselves, the men did as they were told, pushing the horses along the steep slope. Cursing loudly, they fended off low overhang-ing branches, bending low in the saddle.

Suddenly, Corby uttered a low, hissing warning and held up his right hand. In front of them the trees thinned and it was possible to make out the long rocky ledge. Signalling to the men to dismount, he withdrew his Colt and eased his way forward. Crouching behind a tree he let his glance rove over the building, now just visible at the end of the ledge.

There were no lights showing but that meant nothing. The cabin could be completely deserted – or those men were waiting, ready, just behind the two windows. Swiftly, he waved his arm. A thunderous volley of shots rang out, slugs smashing into the thick walls sending chips of wood flying in all directions.

As the booming echoes died away, one of the men called, 'You reckon there's anyone in there, Mr Corby?'

Corby bit his lower lip in indecision. Finally, he made up his mind. 'Three o' you men get ready to bust in. We'll give you coverin' fire.'

A moment later, three men rushed out of the trees towards the cabin. Aiming swiftly, Corby sent several shots in rapid succession through the smashed window. Crouching down against the thick wall, the three men waited. Then one of them ran forward and kicked the door in. Corby saw him step inside.

After a few seconds, the man came out, shaking his head. 'There's no one here.'

Keeping his Colt ready, Corby walked forward, then stepped past the man into the cabin. In the dimness, he could make out little detail. One of the men struck a match and applied it to the wick of the lamp.

'Someone has been here recently,' Corby muttered, struggling to disguise the frustrated disappointment in his tone. 'They can't be far away.'

Going outside, he shouted harshly, 'Half of you men search through these trees. Cover the entire area. I don't care if it takes all night but I want them found. The rest of you get mounted and come with me.'

He knew he had to move quickly if he was to find these men. From the state of the cabin, he estimated they hadn't been gone for long. Clawing his way into the saddle, he led the way down the far side of the hills. Here there were more trees and clumps of tangled undergrowth through which it was difficult to move.

The firs began to thicken the lower they went and all of the men were sweating and cursing by the time they came out onto the edge of the alkali. In the pale light of the westering moon it was possible to see clearly to the distant horizon.

Hauling hard on the reins, Corby brought his mount to a standstill and peered along the edge of the plain searching for any marks which might indicate that his quarry had come this way.

The rest of the men with him paced their mounts slowly in either direction, bending low in the saddle, looking for tell-tale tracks in the white dust. Finally, they returned to where Corby sat waiting.

'Well?' he demanded impatiently.

'Nothing,' grunted one of the men. 'Either they never came this way or they covered their tracks well.' He lifted his glance. 'We'll never find 'em out in the middle of all that alkali.'

'Goddamnit! I intend to find them wherever they are,' Corby snarled. 'All of 'em know far too much, particularly Torbin.'

He noticed the men looking at him with odd expressions on their faces. At the moment, however, he was past caring whether or not they suspected him of having had a hand in the attempt on the judge's life.

'Any of you know what's out there?' he demanded harshly.

'Far as I know,' replied one man, 'there's nothin' but that alkali for thirty miles.'

'You ain't thinking o' ridin' out there, are you, boss?' enquired another. 'A man can get lost in that waste and only the buzzards will find him.'

Corby held himself ramrod straight in the saddle. In his fury at finding nothing, even that thought had crossed his mind. Now, however, common sense took over. Their mounts were tired and having no water with them, it could be suicidal to attempt such a course.

He shook his head. 'If those men back there have found nothin', we'll head back to the ranch. But this ain't the end of it. I know they're out there somewhere and by God, I'll hunt them down if it's the last thing I do.'

'They could be clear over the border by mornin',' suggested the first man.

'There's no chance o' that.' Corby spat the words decisively. 'Kennick will never rest until he's avenged his family. He wants me dead just as much as I aim to see him six feet under the ground.'

'You think those men will bring any more to help us?' Della looked up from her plate, her face just visible in the early morning light. 'They could easily take that money and just ride out.'

Taking out a cigar, Torbin lit it, tossing the spent match on to the ground. 'That was a risk I had to take. I suppose there comes a time when you have to

141

trust someone.' Hitching his gunbelt higher about his waist, he moved towards the door.

'I've known Cy Roberts since I was a kid,' Mark said. 'It hit him hard when Corby took everythin' he had. I'd say he's on the level.'

Torbin came back and seated himself at the table. 'While we're waitin' I reckon we'd better figure out just where and when we hit Corby. A lot is goin' to depend upon if Roberts and the others do bring in any men – and how many there are.'

Calhoun pulled out a chair and sat down. 'Anyone know how many men Corby has?'

Mark pursed his lips. 'Between thirty and forty, I reckon,' he said finally. He eyed Calhoun closely. 'Why – do you have an idea, Frank?'

Calhoun shrugged. 'When you're dealin' with a man like Corby you have to outguess him. It's important we pick the spot where the showdown happens. I'd say it would be foolish to attack him at his spread even though we'd have the advantage of surprise. That place will be like a fortress and him and his men know every bit of it. My guess is we'd be shot to hell before we got near it.'

'Then what do you suggest?' Torbin asked.

The old man gave a grim smile. 'I've been givin' this some thought during the night. We get him to come to us. Even if they come at us from all sides, there's a hell of a lot of open ground they'd have to cross with virtually no cover. With men in all o' these buildings we could cut 'em down before they got near us.'

Torbin considered that for a moment; then

nodded his approval. 'That makes sense. Furthermore he'll only be expectin' four of us.'

'But how do we get him here?' Mark butted in. 'Right now, I doubt if he knows this place exists.'

'That's where you come in. You're goin' to lead him here.'

'And how am I supposed to do that?' Mark stared at him in surprise.

Calhoun lit a cigarette before answering. 'If you were to ride into town and make sure that Corby knows you're there, my guess is he'll gather all of his men and follow you, hopin' you'll lead him to us.'

Mark noticed the sudden expression of alarm on Della's face. Heatedly, she said, 'You're askng Mark to risk his life by doing that. Corby will shoot him on sight.'

Her grandfather shook his head. 'Somehow, I don't think so. It ain't just Mark he wants killed, it's the rest of us. He's no fool, Della. He can't afford to allow the judge here to slip through his fingers and make it back to Twin Springs. That would be the end of him.'

'You willin' to do this, Mark?' Torbin asked seriously.

Mark turned the proposition over in his mind, recognizing that what Calhoun had said made sense. Finally he nodded. 'A lot will depend upon whether Roberts and the others keep their word and get some men to follow 'em – but it seems the only sure way to finish Corby for good.'

'Then it's agreed,' Torbin said. 'Now all we have to do is wait.'

143

It was just after midnight when the sound of approaching riders brought Mark to the door of the adobe dwelling, his Colt in his hand. Moving out into the darkness with the others close behind him, he whispered, 'Can you make out which direction they're comin' from?'

'West,' Torbin said sharply without hesitation. 'I'd say about a dozen of 'em.'

'Then it won't be any o' Corby's men,' Calhoun muttered. 'They'd come from town to the east.'

A few minutes later, they made out the riders. As they approached, a voice called, 'hold your fire.'

Mark instantly recognized Forrester's deep tones. Lowering his weapon, he went forward as the other reined up sharply.

Stepping down, Forrester said hoarsely, 'I managed to get eleven men to ride with me. They're all men handy with their guns.'

'Get their mounts under cover and then bring your men inside,' Torbin ordered. 'Have they been told what we intend to do?'

Forrester gave a brief nod. 'They'll fight so long as they're paid and get the promise of a job once this is finished.'

'What about the others?' Mark asked.

'Last I saw of 'em they were ridin' on to Sioux City close to the border. It's another twenty miles or so. If they're successful, I reckon they should be back within as few hours.'

Slowly, the hours went by. The waiting seemed

interminable but shortly after four o' clock in the morning, Roberts, Clements and Johnson rode in with thirty men at their backs.

'Better get your mounts out o' sight and then somethin' to eat,' Calhoun called. 'It won't be long before there's a showdown here and I want to be sure every man knows exactly what to do.'

'Just who is it we're here to fight?' called one of the men as he led his horse into the deep shadows at the northern end of the village.

'Seth Corby,' Calhoun replied. 'Any o' you men got any problem with that?'

'We fight for whoever pays us,' shouted a second man.

'Then once you're settled in I'll outline the plan.'

The sun had been clear of the horizon for an hour when Mark climbed into the saddle, ready to ride out.

Beside him, Calhoun said quietly, 'You know what to do, Mark. Ride into town and make sure you're seen. Even if Corby ain't there, you can be sure he'll have some of his men around. Give 'em time to get word to him then make your way back here.'

'You're sure he'll fall for this, Frank?'

'I'm sure. At the moment we're a threat to him and Judge Torbin is the biggest. Whatever happens, he can't afford to let the judge live and get word to the federal authorities. He'll be hopin' you'll lead him to us so don't give any indication you know you're bein' trailed.'

'I understand.'

Lifting his glance, Mark saw Della watching him from one of the doorways. She lifted a hand and he could clearly see the anxious look on her face. Then, wheeling his mount with an abrupt pull on the reins, he rode out.

Already, there was a burning heat in the sun. The harsh light reflected cruelly off the white alkali, streaming into his eyes. Outwardly he felt icily calm, yet inwardly his thoughts were in a turmoil. So far, everything had gone as they had planned. With more than forty gunmen to back their play, it seemed nothing could go wrong.

But Corby was an unknown quantity. Utterly ruthless and determined to get everything he wanted, he hadn't got to be the richest and most powerful man in the territory without considering every little detail. He would also be an angry and frustrated man since, so far, his plans had been thwarted at every turn.

A lot was going to depend upon whether he took the bait. Calhoun seemed absolutely certain he would but now, scanning the seemingly endless waste around him, Mark was not so sure. Angry men sometimes did things without thinking of the consequences. Corby may have given the order to have him shot the moment he put in an appearance in town.

Halfway across the arid waste, he turned his mount and headed for the southern edge of the hills. It was a longer route but there was just the possibility that Corby had ridden out to the cabin and left a couple of men behind once he had discovered it to be abandoned.

Meeting up with the main trail an hour later, he slowed his mount to a steady walk. He had the feeling that trouble was about to break although he wasn't sure when it might come and from which direction. The long ravine ahead looked empty but if Corby had any men watching it, they would be well concealed among the heights overlooking it on both sides.

He was almost halfway along it when the shot came. The slug kicked up a spurt of dust in front of his mount. The horse reared as he slid from the saddle. A second gunshot hammered through the silence and this time it came from a slightly different direction.

Narrowing his eyes against the glare of the sunlight, he crouched down behind the stallion. The two drygulchers were holed up among the rocks, keeping out of sight, knowing they had him effectively pinned down. His keen glance, however, had caught a glimpse of the white puff of smoke from the rifle. Now he knew the position of one of the men.

Swiftly, he aimed his Colt and squeezed the trigger twice in rapid succession. He saw the slugs strike the rocks and ricochet away into the distance. Thinning his lips, he assessed his chance of reaching the side of the canyon without being hit. Both of those men would have drawn a bead on him, were waiting for him to make such a move.

A moment later, a harsh voice called, 'Pity we didn't gun you down with the rest o' your family, farmer boy.'

A second voice shouted, 'You've caused us a lot o'

trouble but you ain't goin' to get out o' this.'

Mark clenched his teeth tightly. Although he did not recognize either of the voices, the two men had given their identities away. They were the remaining members of that bunch that had murdered his family!

The sudden realization spurred him into action. Getting his legs under him, he thrust himself forward, weaving from side to side as he headed for the rocks. More shots came from above him, striking the dirt within inches of his feet. Hurling himself forward the last couple of feet, he hit the rocks hard and lay still for a moment, fighting for breath.

No sound came from above him. He guessed the two killers were now waiting for him to show himself, knowing he would have to move out into the open to get off a shot at them. Glancing swiftly to both sides, he noticed the narrow gap in the rocks. Easing himself slowly along the canyon wall, he studied it closely and saw that it stretched all the way to the top.

Raising his voice, he called loudly, 'You're just as yeller as those other skunks who rode with you to shoot down unarmed folk.'

'Then just show yourself, Kennick, and we'll soon see how brave you are.'

The second man uttered a harsh laugh. 'They say you're now mighty fast with a gun,' he yelled.

Mark nodded to himself in satisfaction. Now he knew that the bushwhackers were still there and almost exactly where they were. Sucking in a deep breath, he edged into the gap, using his legs and shoulders to thrust himself up. Sharp rocks caught at his arms and shoulders and in places it seemed too narrow for him to squeeze through.

Five minutes later, with no further sound from his attackers, he succeeded in reaching the top, pulling himself silently onto a flat slab of rock. Easing himself to his feet, pressing his shoulders hard against the rock, he edged forward. A moment later, he spotted the shadow of a man outlined on the stone.

'Where are you, Kennick?' the man yelled a moment later.

'I'm right here,' Mark said softly.

He saw the man suddenly straighten up and whirl swiftly, bringing up his rifle. Before he could utter a sound or squeeze the trigger, Mark's Colt spat gunflame. For a second, the other stood upright, struggling to hold life in his body. Then he lurched drunkenly to one side. His rifle clattered loudly down the slope and an instant later, his body followed it, crashing onto the rocks below.

The second man appeared a few yards away; stunned surprise on his bearded features. Before he could move, Mark fired again. The slug took the man between the eyes, knocking him backward off his feet. His body fell limply across the rocks, his eyes staring sightlessly at the sky.

For a moment, looking down at the two dead men, Mark felt a sense of relief flood through him. At last, he had fulfilled the promise he had made to his father. Now only Seth Corby remained and then his self-imposed task would be finished.

Grim-faced, he edged down the slope to where his

mount stood waiting. Sitting tall in the saddle, he rode into the main street of Henders Rock. Eyeing the boardwalks closely, he noticed that none of Corby's men seemed to be around.

Passing the hardware store, he saw Clayton standing in the doorway shading his eyes against the sunlight. The other saw him at once and his mouth dropped open in sudden surprise. He came forward until he stood beside Mark.

Bending in the saddle, Mark asked in a low voice, 'Is Seth Corby in town, Ed?'

Clayton shook his head. 'Nope. But two o' those killers you were askin' about rode through about half an hour ago.'

'I know. I met up with 'em along the canyon. Neither of 'em will be comin' back.'

'You killed 'em both?' There was undisguised astonishment in Clayton's tone.

'They tried to bushwhack me along the trail. I guess they figured I'd be easy prey.'

The storekeeper hesitated for a moment and then said softly, 'There's word goin' around that Corby has called in all of his men, even those out watchin' the herd. Guess he means trouble. My advice is get out o' town as fast as you can.'

'I'll do that, Ed. Reckon I'll pay a visit to the saloon first.'

Crossing the street, every sense alert for trouble, he pushed open the saloon doors and stepped inside. Before moving up to the bar, he swept his glance over the tables. There were few customers in the saloon at that time of the day and he recognized most of them as townsfolk.

The bartender eyed him curiously as he approached. 'You lookin' to get yourself killed, Mark? I had you figured as bein' well over the border by now, you and that outlaw Calhoun.'

Without turning, Mark asked, 'Any o' Corby's men in, Walt?'

Making a show of mopping the counter with a cloth, the other shook his head. 'Ain't seen any of 'em since yesterday mornin'. Strange that. We usually get one or two of 'em in by now.'

Mark took the whiskey bottle and poured some into the glass. 'Maybe he's got somethin' on his mind – like wonderin' where the circuit judge might be,' Mark said casually.

'You know somethin' about that?' Walt ran his tongue around his lips. 'They say he was taken from the stage and killed.'

'He ain't dead,' Mark told him. 'Right now he's somewhere where Corby won't find him.'

Ten minutes passed. Three of the customers went out. Then the doors opened again and someone came in. Glancing in the mirror, Mark saw the man stare around him. Then his glance fell on Mark. The next second, the man spun on his heel and left, the doors swinging shut behind him.

Behind the counter, the bartender ran his cloth over his forehead. 'That was one o' Corby's ranch hands,' he said hoarsely. 'For a moment I thought he intended to call you out. There ain't no doubt he recognized you.'

Mark gave a grim smile and finished the drink.

'Somehow,' he said thinly, 'I don't think Corby wants me dead – not yet.' Turning, he left the saloon with the barkeep staring bemusedly after him.

CHAPTER VIII

FINAL SHOWDOWN

The afternoon was half over when Mark stepped out of the saloon. By now, he reckoned Corby would have been apprized of his presence in Henders Rock and would be making preparations to trail him once he left town. So far, he thought, Calhoun's hunch had proved correct. Unhitching his mount, he swung into the saddle.

All around him, the street seemed oddly empty. He had half expected Sheriff McKinrick to put in an appearance but there had been no sign of him. Whether he had got wind of Corby's intentions and decided to stay out of things, Mark didn't know. At the moment, his only thought was to ensure that Corby kept him in sight all the way to the adobe village.

With the shadows lengthening around him, he rode through the ravine and then cut across the wasteland towards the rim of the hills. Not until he swung around the side of the high slopes and was partially hidden by a fringe of trees did he risk a quick glance over his shoulder.

At first, he made out nothing. Then, perhaps three miles away, he picked out the cloud of dust. A sense of elation passed momentarily through him as he realized that Corby had taken the bait. With all the men he had at his back, he did not doubt that Corby would be riding with them.

Such was the other's determination to see him and his companions dead that the rancher would want to be in on the final showdown if only to assure himself that, this time, his orders had been carried out. Gigging the stallion forward, he increased his pace a little. There was a little chill on his back as he rode but somehow, he refrained from turning his head again.

Not until he was just a quarter of a mile from the cluster of buildings did he dig spurs into his mount's flanks, sending it racing forward. As he swung from the saddle, Torbin and Calhoun appeared in one of the doorways. There was no sign of the rest of the men or the horses.

'Corby's on his way,' he called, 'two or three miles behind me. From there he can't miss this place.'

'Good,' Torbin said quietly. 'All of the men are in their places and we've moved the horses far enough away so that Corby won't spot them. As far as he knows, there are only four of us here.'

'Did you run into any trouble in town?' Della asked as she came out to stand beside him.

'Two of 'em tried to ambush me on the way there,'

154

he replied soberly. 'They were the last o' that bunch who murdered my parents and sister. I got them both.'

Della nodded. There was a strange look in her eyes. Then she said in a low voice, 'In a way I'm glad you killed them. At least you've avenged your family.'

Mark shook his head. 'Not until Corby is finished.' he muttered through tightly clenched teeth.

'We'd better all get under cover,' her grandfather said thinly. 'Those riders are comin' up fast.' He pointed to where the approaching band was clearly visible. Going inside the building, Mark saw that two of the men the ranchers had brought with them were already crouched down behind the windows.

Torbin stood close by, his back against the wall. At the other window, Mark checked his Colts and then took up his position. Outside, he now saw the riders clearly in the slanting sunlight. A surge of anger passed through him as he made out the familiar figure of Seth Corby in the lead.

Without turning his head, he said, 'Was it wise to put all o' the horses so far away? If Corby figures this ain't going his way he may try to make a run for it.'

'I'd already thought o' that,' Calhoun spoke from the other side of the room. 'There are ten men waiting out there under cover, just in case he does decide to make a break for it. Don't worry, Mark, this time we'll get him.'

Throwing a swift glance around the side of the window, Mark saw that the riders had pulled their mounts to a halt a couple of hundred yards from the perimeter of the village. Corby was talking to one of the men beside him.

Then the rancher lifted his hand. Acting on his command, the men swung round in a large arc. Once they had completely surrounded the cluster of buildings, Corby uttered a loud yell.

Racing their mounts, the attackers surged forward. A moment later, gunfire erupted all around the perimeter. In front of him, Mark saw several of the gunmen topple from their saddles as the withering hail of bullets tore into them. The rest slid from their mounts and threw themselves flat onto the alkali.

Grinning fiercely, he aimed swiftly at a running figure, saw the man stumble and then go down. By now, the attackers had realized they had fallen into a well-executed trap. Slugs hammered against the plaster walls as they returned the fire.

From somewhere out of sight, Corby was yelling, 'Where the hell did all these men come from?'

Echoes of gunfire rolled like thunder on all sides now. The unexpected savagery of the defence had taken all of Corby's men by surprise. Now they were struggling to find whatever cover they could from the vicious crossfire that came from every window.

More of the attackers died, caught in the open. The rest, however, continued to pour gunfire against the building, knowing the futility of attempting to make for their mounts. One of the men at the far window suddenly slumped back with a moaning cry as a bullet took him in the head.

Without pausing to think, Della moved across to take his place. Gritting his teeth, Mark shifted a little to the side as he spotted two men stumbling to their feet. Turning they ran back towards the horses. Almost without taking conscious aim, Mark lifted his Colts and pressed both triggers simultaneously.

One of the men threw up his arms as if clawing at the sky. He stood there for a moment, somehow remaining upright on his feet. Then his back arched and he dropped forward, rolling onto his side. The second man had half-turned when the slug hit him in the side, burying itself deep within his body.

Narrowing his eyes, Mark lifted his gaze. Colby was still seated on his mount, staring wildly about him, an expression of utter disbelief on his face. Seeing him, all of the old anger and hatred swept through Mark. An image of his sister running from the house only to fall with a bullet in her back flashed through his mind.

He knew that the rancher was too far away for a killing shot from a revolver. Yet at any moment he knew that Corby would now attempt to flee, seeing his dreams of empire fading before his eyes.

Almost without thinking, Mark ran across the room to where Della knelt behind the far window. Without a word, he snatched the Winchester from her hand, saw the expression of startled surprise on her face. Swiftly, he checked it, then moved towards the door.

Behind him, he heard Calhoun's shout of warning but in his anger he ignored it. Stepping outside, he called loudly, his voice rising above the diminishing sound of gunfire. 'Seth Corby!'

He saw the rancher turn his head and knew that

the other had seen him. For a moment, Corby made no move. Then his right hand dropped towards the rifle beside him. Jerking it from its scabbard, he raised it, sighting the barrel on Mark.

Holding the Winchester in both hands, Mark fired from the hip. For a moment, he thought the bullet had missed. Corby remained upright, staring at Mark across the intervening distance.

Then the rifle fell from his hands as he fell forward across the neck of his mount. Wildly, the stallion pawed momentarily at the air, throwing Corby's inert body onto the alkali. Mark stood quite still. Around him, only a few desultory shots continued. When the silence fell it seemed almost as deafening as the racketing gunfire.

Torbin stood up. To Calhoun, he said tersely, 'Get some o' the men to check if there are any of Corby gunslicks still on their feet and we'll take them back into jail. With Corby dead, I don't think McKinrick will have any objections to keeping 'em under lock and key until I try them.'

As he went out, Calhoun threw Mark a meaningful glance. 'That was some o' the best shootin' I've seen with a rifle,' he remarked.

Moving towards him out of the dimness, Della took the Winchester from him. She said softly, 'Somehow, now all of this is finished, I don't think you'll be needing this again.'

A moment later, Torbin came to stand beside them in the doorway. He glanced round as Della asked, 'What will happen to my grandfather, Judge? Do you have to take him in for trial?'

Torbin wiped some of the gunsmoke and dust from his face. 'Somehow, I reckon that after the federal authorities hear what I have to say, both your grandfather and you, Mark, will have that brand removed from your hides.'

He paused for a moment to take a cigar from his waistcoat pocket. 'My advice to you, Mark, is to go back and start rebuilding that spread o' yours. You've finished what you set out to do and with Corby gone there'll be law and order now in Henders Rock.'

Mark nodded. 'I guess you're right, Judge. It'll seem strange working the place all on my own but—'

He felt a light touch on his arm and turned to find Della looking up at him. There was a smile on her face and a look in her eyes he had never seen before. Softly, she said, 'That's something you don't have to do, Mark. A place like that needs a woman's touch.'

Drawing his head down to hers, he felt the soft touch of her lips on his. Walking up to the doorway, Calhoun made to say something, then stopped. Throwing a meaningful glance at Torbin, he walked away to see to the horses.